The Author

MARIAN ENGEL was born in Toronto, Ontario, in 1933. She grew up in the Ontario towns of Brantford, Galt, Hamilton, and Sarnia. She received her B.A. (1955) from McMaster University and her M.A. (1957) from McGill University, where she wrote her thesis, "The Canadian Novel, 1921-55," under the supervision of Hugh MacLennan.

After living abroad and teaching in the United States and Europe, Engel returned to Canada in 1964 and settled in Toronto, which she made the setting of her novels.

Her many novels and short stories explore the daily lives of her characters, particularly reflecting upon the human condition from the perspective of women.

Engel was a founding member of the Writers' Union of Canada and served as its first chairman in 1973-74.

Marian Engel died in Toronto in 1985.

THE NEW CANADIAN LIBRARY

General Editor: David Staines

MARIAN ENGEL

Bear

With an Afterword by Aritha van Herk

M&S

The following dedication appeared in the original edition:

for John Rich
who knows how animals think

Copyright © 1976 by Marian Engel
Afterword copyright © 1990 by Aritha van Herk

This book was first published by
McClelland and Stewart Limited in 1976.

Reprinted May 1990

Canadian Cataloguing in Publication Data

Engel, Marian, 1933 – 1985
Bear

(New Canadian library)
ISBN 0-7710-9958-4

I. Title. II. Series.

PS8559.N5B42 1990   C813'.54   C90-093063-2
PR9199.3.E54B42 1990

Printed and bound in Canada

McClelland & Stewart Inc.
The Canadian Publishers
481 University Avenue
Toronto, Ontario
M5G 2E9

The author acknowledges with thanks the Canada Council and the Arts Council of Ontario, who provided funds while this book was in progress.

The author is grateful for the bibliographical assistance of Dr. Robert Brandeis, librarian at Huron College, London, Ontario.

"Facts become art through love, which unifies them and lifts them to a higher plane of reality; and in landscape, this all-embracing love is expressed by light."

Kenneth Clark,
Landscape into Art

I

In the winter, she lived like a mole, buried deep in her office, digging among maps and manuscripts. She lived close to her work and shopped on the way between her apartment and the Institute, scurrying hastily through the tube of winter from refuge to refuge, wasting no time. She did not like cold air on her skin.

Her basement room at the Institute was close to the steam pipes and protectively lined with books, wooden filing cabinets and very old, brown, framed photographs of unlikely people: General Booth and somebody's Grandma Town, France from the air in 1915, groups of athletes and sappers; things people brought her because she would not throw them out, because it was her job to keep them.

"Don't throw it out," people said. "Lug it all down to the Historical Institute. They might want it.

11

He might have been more of a somebody than we thought, even if he did drink.'' So she had retrieved from their generosity a Christmas card from the trenches with a celluloid boot on it, a parchment poem to Chingacousy Township graced with a wreath of human hair, a signed photograph of the founder of a seed company long ago absorbed by a competitor. Trivia which she used to remind herself that long ago the outside world had existed, that there was more to today than yesterday with its yellowing paper and browning ink and maps that tended to shatter when they were unfolded.

Yet, when the weather turned and the sun filtered into even her basement windows, when the sunbeams were laden with spring dust and the old tin ashtrays began to stink of a winter of nicotine and contemplation, the flaws in her plodding private world were made public, even to her, for although she loved old shabby things, things that had already been loved and suffered, objects with a past, when she saw that her arms were slug-pale and her fingerprints grained with old, old ink, that the detritus with which she bedizened her bulletin boards was curled and valueless, when she found that her eyes would no longer focus in the light, she was always ashamed, for the image of the Good Life long ago stamped on her soul was quite different from this, and she suffered in contrast.

This year, however, she was due to escape the shaming moment of realization. The mole would not be forced to admit that it had been intended for an antelope. The Director found her among her files and rolled maps and, standing solemnly under a row of family portraits donated to the Institute on the grounds that it would be impious to hang them, as was then fashionable, in the bathroom, announced that the Cary estate had at last been settled in favour of the Institute.

He looked at her, she looked at him: it had happened. For once, instead of Sunday school attendance certificates, old emigration documents, envelopes of unidentified farmers' Sunday photographs and withered love letters, something of real value had been left them.

"You'd better get packing, Lou," he said, "and go up and do a job on it. The change will do you good."

Four years before, they had received a letter from a firm of lawyers in Ottawa stating that the residue of the estate of Colonel Jocelyn Cary, including Cary Island, the estate thereon known as Pennarth, and the contents of its buildings, had been left to the Institute. The lawyers added that they understood that Pennarth contained a large library of materials relevant to early settlement in the area.

Lou and the Director searched their files for references to Cary, and sent researchers over to the Provincial Archives. They unearthed a file in the archaic handwriting of Miss Bliss, Lou's predecessor, regarding a visit from one Colonel Jocelyn Cary, in 1944, during the course of which the bequest was proposed. The Director had been overseas at the time; the Institute impoverished. Nothing was done to follow up the offer, and by the time Lou got her growing-up over with and came to work at the Institute, Miss Bliss had long ago taken to drink and larded her files with many impossible suggestions.

"Well," said the Director cautiously, "we'd better not get our hopes up. It's never happened before."

The relatives sued, of course. Cary Island, they had all found out, was no longer an isolated outpost on a lonely river; it had been transformed by automobiles, motorboats, long holidays, and snowmobiles and cash to real estate.

While the Director wangled legal assistance at the Provincial Government's expense (for the Institute had gradually been taken over), Lou dug and devilled in library and files, praying as she worked that research would reveal enough to provide her subject with a character. The Canadian tradition was, she had found, on the whole, genteel. Any evidence that an ancestor had performed any acts other than working and praying was usually destroyed. Families handily became respectable in retrospect but it was, as she and the Director often mourned, hell on history. If Cary had had enough money and enough energy to build a house that far north, and fill it with books, he was unusual. It was up to her to find out how unusual he was, and in the meantime to pray to whatever gods, muses and members of Parliament overlooked the affairs of the Institute that enough would be revealed to develop the dim negative of that region's history.

The Colonel Cary who made the bequest had included an outline of his ancestor's accomplishments. It appeared that the old Colonel, born the year of the outbreak of the French Revolution to a good but untitled Dorset family, had been sent for a soldier at an early age and served in Portugal and Sicily during the Napoleonic wars. At the age of twenty, he had married a Miss Arnold, whose father was adjutant of the troops stationed at Messina. He had risen in the ranks of the artillery, bred a number of children on his wife, served with distinction in a number of campaigns in the Po valley and returned to England with his brood at the end of the wars – unemployed.

All this information had been verified by references to land titles, commissions, military recommendations and citations.

During his military service, the descendant noted, the Colonel had become attached to the idea of living on an island. The family legend was that one hot summer, stationed on Malta, he opened an atlas of the New World, closed his eyes, and picked out Cary Island with a pin.

Lou thought of him sitting on a portable military thunderbox groaning with summer dysentery, longing for cool water. No pin was necessary. After a futile search for employment in England, he sold what property he owned there and moved with his family to Toronto, then York, in 1826.

Good. He was in the records. Cary. Colonel John William. Shuter Street, number 22. Gentleman.

It was not until 1834 that he obtained the charter ('Your petitioner humbly sheweth . . .') to settle Cary Island, having promised to build a lumbermill and provide a sailing ship for trade in the region.

"My grandmother," wrote the descendant, "however, refused to go further into the wilderness and face the inclemencies of the north. She was meridional in temperament, if not in ancestry. The Colonel was forced to leave her behind in York with her daughters and the younger sons. He went north with his second son Rupert (I believe the oldest, Thomas Bedford Cary, was delicate, as he was buried in 1841 in the

Necropolis Cemetery) and lived on the island very simply for the rest of his life."

Official references to Cary were scant. His petition for settlement of Cary Island and later his outright purchase, funded by the sale of his commission, were recorded. According to city directories, Mrs. Henrietta Cary continued to live in York at respectable addresses long after it was named Toronto. The Colonel was appointed Magistrate for the Northern District in 1836.

And given a military funeral at Sault Ste Marie in 1869 at the age of ninety.

It was the years on Cary Island that Lou was to research and discover now. For the Institute had won its suit with costs and she was detailed to inspect the property this summer. It was only a matter, the lawyers and the caretakers of the property advised, of waiting until the weather was such that she would feel comfortable at Pennarth, which had never had central heating.

II

On the fifteenth of May she loaded her car with filing folders, paper, cards, notebooks and a typewriter. She had rooted out her old camping gear — motheaten mackinaw jackets, hiking boots, a juvenile sleeping-bag. The Director offered her a farewell handshake and drew back from the smell of mothballs.

"Your man is called Homer Campbell. You turn off Highway 17 at Fisher's Falls and follow county road 6 to a village called Brady. Turn left at the crossroads there, and follow the river shore until you get to Campbell's Marina. Homer will fix you up with a boat and take you to the island. I was talking to him yesterday. He says he's connected up a new tank of propane and had someone clean the house for you."

The road went north. She followed it. There was a Rubicon near the height of land. When she crossed it, she began to feel free. She sped north to the highlands, lightheaded.

The lawyers' inventory of the house and outbuildings indicated that she would not have much need for equipment. The house was no log cabin. It had six rooms, one of which was a library. There were many sofas, many tables, many chairs. She could see their spread legs as they sat on the list. She felt everything was going to be comfortable.

The land was hectic with new green. Crossing the bay, she shivered on the deck of the car ferry that connected the parts of the broken limestone arch of islands. Gulls wheeled and in the distance a foghorn blew. She passed one big island she had longed to live on all her life, and a little one, supposed by the Indians to be haunted, that she had been taken to as a child. She remembered going out to it in a big cruiser, landing, finding the paths obscured by poison ivy plants as tall as herself. Her parents were looking for fringed gentians and grass of Parnassus. While they searched she found herself riveted by the skeleton of the biggest dragonfly in the world, caught in a spiderweb in a cabin window, sucked dry.

Little islands floated innocently on the waves, rocked by bell-buoys.

There were not many passengers aboard at this time of year: a few hunters, a couple of Indians in magenta ski jackets, an elderly couple reading side by side at the top of the companionway. A French-speaking family in new pastel sporting clothes. The tradition that everything for outdoors must be soiled and pilled and forty years old seemed to have died except in her. She thought of a man she knew who said it was now impossible to find a woman who smelled of her own self.

It was nearly dusk when they pulled into the ferry dock. She had sharp memories of being here before. She remembered a beach, a lake the colour of silver, something sad happening. Something, yes, that happened when she was very young, some loss. It struck her as strange that she had never come back to this part of the world.

While she waited for her car to be driven off, she watched the Indians getting into a new white panel truck.

It was too late to make the marina before dark, for the trek on the ferry was, as usual, time-consuming. She took a room in a motel on a deserted beach, spent the evening mooching along the water, listening to the birds.

"I have an odd sense," she wrote on a postcard to the Director, "of being reborn."

Driving off the island the next morning, she felt her heart lurch at the sight of the bald stone mountains of Algoma. Where have I been? she wondered. Is a life that can now be considered an absence a life?

For some time things had been going badly for her. She could cite nothing in particular as a problem; rather, it was as if life in general had a grudge against her. Things persisted in turning grey. Although at first she had revelled in the erudite seclusion of her job, in the protection against the vulgarities of the world that it offered, after five years she now felt that in some way it had aged her disproportionately, that she was as old as the yellowed papers she spent her days unfolding. When, very occasionally, she raised her eyes from the past and surveyed the present, it faded from her view and became as ungraspable as a mirage. Although she had discussed this with the Director, who waved away her condition of mind as an occupational hazard, she was still not satisfied that this was how the only life she had been offered should be lived.

It was late when she parked by the marina. She went into the cement-block store and asked for Homer Campbell. The round-faced storekeeper admitted his identity.

"You'll be the lady from the Institute Mr. Dickson was writing me about," he said. "You made good time. We can go over tonight." He called his son and began unloading her car immediately. When she fussed a little about the typewriter, he shot her a look of pity.

He was middle-aged and cheerful. His son Sim was pale-eyed, pale-haired, a ghost, an albino, silently loading a second motorboat with boxes of supplies they had ready for her. He spoke to his son in chirps and clucks as he would to an animal. The son was big-footed, bashful, passive: fifteen, fourteen, she concluded.

She found it awkward getting seated in the motorboat: she seemed not to know how to bend anymore. Homer tried to show her how to start the motor, but she felt very far away.

She had studied the water-charts. She knew Cary's island was several miles up the reedy river-mouth they were penetrating. It was a likely-looking place on a map, but she already knew that the Colonel had not taken into account the fact that the river, for all its wide mouth, petered out to a stream further up, so that his marshy haven was more isolated than a cartographer would have reason to expect. His lumbermill had failed, she had read, because the elegant, English-looking river supplied only enough water to turn the wheel a day a week.

Homer talked loudly at her over the motor's roar. He seemed a loquacious man. She was more interested in the magical forms around her, the way rock ruggedness quickly converted to sand and birch, and islands no bigger than sandbars were crowned with shuttered old green cottages that looked lost and abandoned at this time of year. In this country, she thought, we have winter lives and summer lives of completely different quality.

They slid down the chilly channel, Sim in a silver boat trailing behind them.

"You're not so far out," Homer shouted. "You'll want to keep gas in the tank in case you need help, though. You won't likely have no trouble with storms this time of year but you could get a lightning strike or a bad throat or something. Joe King lives over there when he has his traplines out in the winter, and his auntie, Mrs. Leroy, she's an old Indian woman, she's over on Neebish with her niece, so you won't have no unexpected company.

"There's a woodstove and a gas stove and a couple of fireplaces. They had a space heater Joe and I took out, it was damn dangerous. Joe's filled your woodshed, the old woman swep' the place out for you, you'll be snug as a bug in a rug. If she comes back, you'll know her. She's as old as the hills and she's got no teeth."

The boat was an old cedar strip outboard, but the motor was new. Homer assured her it wouldn't leak so much once it had spent a little time in the water. There was a canoe in the boathouse; he didn't know what shape it was in. He'd put a light motor of his own on the boat, figuring she wouldn't want to haul the big twenty horse-power up to the house when the weather got bad. Main thing was to keep it clean and dry, and keep the gas-can full.

An enormous foghorn sounded. In spite of herself, she jumped. Homer laughed. "Sounds like a cow bellowing right up in your ear, don't it? The shipping channel's only four, five miles the other side of your place. We'll have a good year. The river's open early."

So this silent, creeping shore was Cary's island. Sedge at the shore, then anonymous stones and trees. "There's the point. We'll round it in a minute." There was something affectionate in Homer's voice, as if he loved the place. He looked at her, and looked away.

When they were around the riverbend, he pointed, and she saw the house looming white against the darkening sky. She sucked in her breath and waited; then, when they were close to the dock she saw that what she had thought was true: the house was a classic Fowler's octagon.

"Wow," she said.

"Pretty fine, isn't it?"

"It's not mentioned in the textbooks. There's an index of houses like that."

"Oh, we're pretty cagey, up here. Nobody would know about this place who wasn't running around in a boat; and none of us are telling. We send all the tourists down to gaggle at that house Longfellow was supposed to have written that Indian poem in, down there in the main channel. This place has been forgotten about, sort of, and around here we think it's just as well. It's a dilly, isn't it? Wait til you come up the river on your own on a July morning. Nothing like it. Get the rope, Sim."

They tied up at a small dock, and Sim and Homer had the boat half unloaded before she was properly on her feet.

"The relatives were fit to be tied when it was left to your outfit," Homer went on. "Wanted the whole island shucked up in cottage lots. Government won't allow that any more. Here, come on up and I'll show you inside."

Staggering under the weight of her suitcases, she followed Homer up the bank, over a wide green lawn ('Sim here will mow her for you') to the verandah of the house.

"Hope you can manage without electric light," Homer said. "There's a couple of gas lights but they're none too bright. You'll need to work in a window. Plenty of windows, though."

She stood gazing at the house, letting his words slip after her. In the dusk, it was a gentle bulk. Its wide verandahs dimmed the windows of the ground floor. High trees arched over them.

"Black birch," Homer said. "There's something special about those trees: it's cooler under them than anywhere on a hot August day."

"I don't know that I'll be here til August," she murmured.

"Nobody ever left this place that didn't have to. That granddaughter in Cleveland would have given her eye teeth for it. Spent thousands trying to keep it from going to your outfit. Here, I've got the keys."

23

It was so long since she had seen a long, toothed house key that she had forgotten what it was called.

"Didn't need to lock up before the snowmobilers came," Homer said. "You win some, you lose some." Their footsteps sounded hollow on the porch.

Homer opened the front door. She stepped inside and put her bags down in the front hall. She was surrounded by doors and windows. Ahead of her was a broad stairwell leading to the top of the house.

Smell of stove oil. Smell of mice. Smell of dust (last sun slanting low through small old window-panes). Homer stood almost apologetically beside her, looking for her smile of approval. She looked up the stairs, to the left, to the right, and sniffed. Another smell, musky, unidentifiable but good. Homer turned to the right, opened the door, and laid her big type-writer on a table in a dim room. The boy came with the duffle bags. Plonk. Plunk. He went back for more.

"These houses are more or less round," Homer said. "You come with me and I'll show you around. Know how to light a kerosene lamp?"

"Yes."

"Show me." An elaborate milk-glass lamp hung from the ceiling of the room she was in, but from somewhere else Homer produced a tin lantern like a railwayman's. She lit it, and the room leapt into a glow of sofas and bow-legged tables, plant-stands and dead ferns. "You'll be more interested in the kitchen. It's through here. Remember the dampers on a wood stove?"

"No."

"When you've had the grand tour I'll show you.

24

You'll need it for a little heat in the morning. You could still get snow up here, you know."

The kitchen took only one plane of the octagon, as opposed to the parlour's two. There was a modern propane stove beside the wood stove, a roll-top kitchen machine, and a tin sink with a pump.

"There's a better one outside," Homer said. "We always had trouble with the leathers on this one. Now this next room's a sort of combination woodshed and back hall, leads out to the real woodshed. There's a yard out there, and a backhouse. Lucy's cleaned the place up real good, hasn't she? In here, this next room's the master bedroom, like. The bed looks kinda saggy. She's laid you a fire. Here, I'll light it for you, and take you along out back and show you what's where. Come out the front door and around. The back steps are bad at night."

It was considerably darker now, and the air was damp and chilly. She shivered as she followed Homer around the south side of the house, where he showed her the long-handled outdoor pump, and the out-house that was one of a collection of sheds off the back yard. It was a two-holer and she noticed with amusement that its seat-covers were old-fashioned enamel streetlight reflectors pinch-frilled like pie-edges.

She made as if to go inside the house again, for it was dark and she was tired and cold, but Homer stood looking at her uneasily, shifting from foot to foot. She wondered if he was going to touch her or to denounce her. She wanted to get in and get settled. There had been so much day; she had a lot to think about. She was impatient.

"Did anyone tell you," he asked, "about the bear?"

III

There had always, it seemed, been a bear. That Lord
Byron the first Colonel was so stuck on had kept a
bear. The Colonel kept a bear. There was still a bear.
Joe King's aunty, Lucy Leroy, a hundred years old, if
you could believe them, looked after the bear after the
Colonel died. But she was gone. It was out back now.
It would be asleep. But she ought to know about the
bear.

"I don't hold any brief for bears. I don't like pet
animals much, to tell the truth. I like a dog if he's a
good retriever, and the odd time I've taken in some
critter that's been hurt but the Carys had this thing
about keeping a bear and when the Colonel died
what could you do about it? There it was. So without
saying much to the lawyers we kept it. Joe and Lucy
took care of it. It's got a shed of its own back there —
the original log house. You're from Toronto, you'll

26

love a log house. It's kind of an old bear, but not too bad-tempered.

"I didn't know what to do when they said they were sending a woman up here. I'd expected a man, I dunno why.

"It's there, and it belongs to the place. I don't know where they got it, there aren't any bear around here. Maybe Lucy knows, but she went off to her daughter-in-law. I didn't know what the hell to say to you about it, but you look all right. You treat it like a dog, Joe said. I asked him before he went away. But don't get too friendly before the bear knows you because he's kind of old, nobody remembers how old, but they live to twenty-five or thirty so he can't be too young. I came right back here after the war, and I can't remember a cub, but of course I wasn't here much. Cary didn't like company except an order of groceries once in a while.

"Joe's left a hundred pounds of dog chow in the shed. Whatever else is there came out of the money the Institute sent us when they said you were coming.

"I don't know what I'd do if anybody laid a bear on my shoulders. All I can say is, Lucy says he's a good bear and you know some people don't like Indians and they can't hold their liquor, but around here we respect Lucy, and if she says it's a good bear, maybe I can ask you to feed it and water it while you're here and after that we'll decide what to do."

Having spoken quickly and nervously, he looked towards the dark trees at the back of the lighted house, shook his head, put his hand on her upper arm, and guided her up the verandah steps. At the front door he said that she ought to try to come over to the marina by herself in the motorboat tomorrow. If she didn't arrive by four, he'd come over and see what the matter was. The trick was to turn left when the river mouth opened into the main channel.

Then he called his son and beat it.

IV

She went inside and sat down, dazed, at the kitchen table. She heard the sound of the motorboat going away, then nothing. She opened two doors so she could see the crackling fire in her bedroom. So this was her kingdom: an octagonal house, a roomful of books, and a bear.

She could not take it in. She was stunned by it. There must be a word for such a wildly happy find — joy, luck, whatever it was come by chance: ah, serendipity. Without giving up her work (which she loved), she was deposited in one of the great houses of the province, at the beginning of the summer season and in one of the great resort areas. She was somewhat isolated, but she had always loved her loneliness. And the idea of the bear struck her as joyfully Elizabethan and exotic.

She lit the gas-lamp in the kitchen easily enough: held a match to it, turned its key, and heard it pop softly alight. Under its warm glow she filled the kettle with a dipper from a graniteware pail of water by the sink. The water was cold and smelled of sulphur. The house was cold now too.

She made herself a cup of tea and took it into the dim bedroom, where she sat on a long, curving sofa in front of the fire, staring into the flames. By what crazy luck she had come to this place she would never know. "I will be happy," she whispered to herself.

One of her country uncles used to say when his luck turned good, "I'm sitting with my feet in a tub of butter."

Her feet were cold. She took off her boots and toasted her socks at the fire. Half stretched out, she realized she was exhausted: joy was tiring. She rummaged in her baggage for her sleepingbag and laid it out on the sofa. The colonel's huge bed behind her looked both formidable and damp. She tidied the kitchen, turned out the light, unhooked her brassiere, and slid fully dressed into the sleepingbag. Still listening to the fire, she fell asleep.

She woke early. She was cold. Very cold. She pulled her sweater down and her sleepingbag up, wriggled until she was comfortable, and prepared to go to sleep again. Meanwhile, she sniffed the cold, fresh air and remembered where she was. The house smelled of woodsmoke and new grass.

At seven, she got up and put her boots on; went outside to survey her kingdom.

It was a grand one. A hundred yards of river front had been turned into wide, just-greening lawns. Along the bank stood a row of magnificent, evenly

30

spaced maple trees coming into flower. Beyond them, the river stretched silver, curling around its shoals, and disappeared into scrawny birch and brush again. There was no sign of any other habitation.

She stood on the riverbank quite still, conscious that every motion made a foreign sound, even her hands rubbing in her pockets for warmth. She savoured the newness around her, the yellow wands of scrub willow at the edge of the bush, the listing boathouse, the green buds of the trees, then turned to face the incredible house.

Its faceted white bulk gleamed in the early sun; its black-roofed verandahs hung like an apron over the first floor. The windows of the second storey were broad and shining. From its roof, two chimneys and a windowed lantern rose like the crown of a hat. She could hardly believe its perfection.

Then she remembered the bear. This was not a dream. That man, that man Homer, had told her that behind the house there was a bear. It has seemed a wonderfully strange idea at first, but it appeared there really was a bear. By now, patently a hungry bear. She ought to go and look. There was no use avoiding it.

She wondered if the bear would be good company.

V

She was not fond of animals. Had had a puppy once and been much moved when he was run over, but had not missed him. Had been annoyed by kittens but rather pleased by calves on a farm she visited once. That was her history. A dubious beginning for a bear.

So, she thought, maybe I'll start on the books first, work from the known to the unknown; but she had also to go out to the outhouse, which was in the same direction as his shed. She plucked up her courage. If she could not face the animal she might take some interest in the chinking and notching of his shelter.

From the front, the house looked single and solitary, but there was a fungus of outbuildings behind it: a board and batten woodshed, and a tumbledown log house connected to it by something that looked like a corncrib and was perhaps a wood shelter of the remains of a chicken house. Together, they formed a fenced compound.

She approached this compound by its southward gate. The bear would be in the old cabin. There was a post by the door and on the post a chain which disappeared into darkness. The ground was muddy, but there were no new tracks in the mud. What do you say to a bear? she wondered, leaning on the fence.

"Hello," she said softly into the darkness. She got no reply. It must be asleep, she thought; maybe it's still hibernating.

The time she had met a moose was the only time she had felt her knees knocking. She had expected to be afraid of the bear, but here she was standing quite calmly in his doorway. She was certain that it was there, and that it was benevolent. She wondered what kind of fool she was.

She went back into the house, slamming the screen door behind her. There was a great deal to do before she could do what she wanted — start on the books — because if she did not unpack now she would live her life here in a muddle. First she organized her personal possessions in the bedroom, then she loaded the canned goods haphazardly into the kitchen cupboards. It took her a long time to decide what to do with refrigerator things like butter and bacon. She found a rusty four-sided toaster and put it over the gas element. She wiped a black iron frying pan out and laid strips of bacon in it. She was hungry.

The morning light was dappled, fallow, green, a moving presence at the windows. The kitchen swam in an underwater gloom. When her breakfast was cooked, she carried it out to the stoop of the woodshed

33

to sit in the light. As she sat down, she realized the bear was standing in his doorway staring at her.

Bear. There. Staring.

She stared back.

Everyone has once in his life to decide whether he is a Platonist or not, she thought. I am a woman sitting on a stoop eating bread and bacon. That is a bear. Not a toy bear, not a Pooh bear, not an airlines Koala bear. A real bear.

Half a bear, actually, and not a very big half, for it lay tentatively in his doorway so that she had no idea of its size. It was only a dusty bulk of blackish fur in a doorway. It had a long brown snout, and its snout had a black, dry, leathery end. It had small, sad eyes.

They stared at each other as she ate, sizing each other up. It was no less small-eyed when it turned full face towards her: its gaze was not direct; it was diffused by the angles of its skull. This long, brown snout and these small eyes turned towards her. It did not seem menacing, only tired and sad. The only sign of animation was a quivering of the nostrils at the sound of her fork on the enamel plate.

She thought, you have these ideas about bears: they are toys, or something fierce and ogreish in the woods, following you at a distance, snuffling you out to snuff you out. But this bear is a lump.

Then, because the one thing she knew about animals was their enormous and, it seemed to her, parasitical hunger, she went into the shed and scooped dry food from a sack into the basin that sat beside it. This she took gingerly to the bear. It looked perhaps a little brighter as it quickly curved an arm out and pulled the basin to it, and put its jaws inside.

Then it looked up to her again, as if for permission. No, she thought, more likely it wants me to go away.

She watched it from a distance while it gorged noisily. When it had finished, it looked up at her and licked its nose with a long, thin, ant-eater's tongue. Then it licked its chops with a tongue that seemed to have become short and fat. Then, with what seemed a very great effort, it hauled itself on all fours, and advanced towards her.

She sucked in her breath and stood quite, quite, still, forbidding her knees to knock a second time.

The bear stood in the open, on all fours, and stared at her, moving its head up, down, and sideways to get a full view of her. Its nose was more pointed than she had expected — years of corruption by teddy bears, she supposed — and its eyes were genuinely piggish and ugly. She crossed the yard and pumped it a pail of water.

She set the pail down quite near it, nearer than she thought she ought to have dared, but the bear looked so passive she could not genuinely fear it. In its stable doorway, it had looked smaller. Now she could see that it was what Homer would call a good size: up to her hip and long with it; a full-grown bear with a scruff like a widow's hump.

As it turned to drink, she got a large whiff of shit and musk. It was indubitably male, she saw, and its hindquarters were matted with dirt. After it drank thirstily, it curled up again by the barn door. It looked stupid and defeated. She hunkered where it could not reach her and stared at it. Its nose was like a dog's but broader. Its snout was narrow, its eyes were close together. It was not a handsome beast. And it would not be, if it always lived at the end of that chain. She thought briskly of restoring some gloss to it, taking it for walks.

"Bear," she whispered to it, "who and what are you?"

Bear did not reply, but turned its head toward her with a look of infinite weariness, and closed its eyes. She sat for a long time smoking, drinking coffee, staring at it. She had taken some nephews to a bad movie about bears once. That was all.

An unprepossessing creature, this bear, she decided. Not at all menacing. Not a creature of the wild, but a middle-aged woman defeated to the point of being daft, who had sat night after night waiting for her husband for so long that time had ceased to exist and there was only waiting. I can manage him, she decided, and went inside.

She washed her dishes, spent some time rearranging the kitchen cupboards to suit her left-handedness, exclaiming to herself over the kitchen dishes, which should not in such a place have been anything other than willow pattern, and were not, and, knowing further delay was only delicious procrastination, moved slowly through the arc of the house, parlour to hall, and stood at the foot of the stairs.

A house like this, she thought, in these regions was an absurdity; too elaborate, too hard to heat, no matter how much its phrenological designer thought it good for the brain. To build such a place in the north, among log houses and sturdy square farmhouses, was colonial pretentiousness. She shivered as she thought of the open stairwell in howling winter. When he sold these plans, Fowler had recommended.

a construction of a homemade stucco that turned out to be as durable as flypaper. He was the sort of American we are all warned about.

She went up towards the light, complaining in her practical mind about immigrant idiocies. Stopped dead at the top of the stairs in a blaze of sunshine.

The two chimneys hemmed the stairwell. Over it gleamed an enormous windowed lantern. Aside from that, the second floor was open. Four walls were windowed to the height of built-in counters; the other four were papered with glassed bookshelves. There were vast sofas in front of the fireplaces and low tables stacked with folio-sized books. An elaborate brass Tilley lamp hung over the counter facing the river. The windows were shaded with nautical-looking rolled-up canvas blinds.

From the front window the river had another dimension. She could see it idling all the way to the river channel.

She stood quietly, fingering the brass and leather telescope on the sill, dusting with empty fingers the celestial and terrestial globes on either side of it. If the books were all bad Boston Bunyans, she did not want to know yet. She went to the table by the northern fireplace and opened a volume of engravings of ruins. Piranesi. She stared at the broken columns for a long time. Then she went and looked out the back window, brushing a dead fly off the empty counter. The bear was staring up at her.

She waded around the room slowly, reverently. It was a sea of gold and green light.

She wondered where to begin, and indulged herself by lazily scanning the shelves trying to comprehend the books' scope and order. She was presented with a sharp and perhaps typical early nineteenth-century mind: Encyclopaedias, British and Greek history, Voltaire, Rousseau, geology and geography, geophysical speculation, the more practical philosophers, sets and sets of novelists. She wondered where else there was such a perfect library for its period. She had no fear that her work would not consume a summer.

She went downstairs and brought up her paper, her typewriter, her filing cards. She sat down immediately and tapped out a letter to the Director telling him that all was well. Then she looked at her watch and discovered it was time to leave for Homer's store.

VI

She was still trying to find the snap of the elbow that would whip the motor to life when Homer veered around the point and drew up beside her. She looked at him in daylight. He had a shrewd face, round pink-framed plastic glasses, very false false teeth, little broken veins in his cheeks. He wore a green drill workman's cap and a red mackinaw. She liked him.

After he showed her again the knack of getting the engine going, she followed him down the channel. He yelled back to her that the water was low this year, and told her the names of the shoals and asked did she know the difference between a shoal and an island? It had to have a tree to be an island. That was important up here.

That island there was where old Mrs. Bird was found almost dead one spring among her eleven children. Her husband had gone out across the ice for supplies in January, must have fallen through. She and the children survived the winter on turnips. They were okay but she was in hospital so long the Children's Aid had to farm out all the kids, and only one ever came back to see her, though she lived to be ninety-four. People still do get lost, he said, winters when the ice is punky.

Homer's grocery store left a sophisticated taste something to desire, but contained the necessities. It made her glad she had grown up on Campbell's soup and bologna and peanut butter sandwiches. He sold withered potatoes, knobby carrots and wilted cabbages, but good local cheese and pale, creamy butter. He apologized for the vegetables. "I have to get the stuff up from Toronto and it don't keep. You'll have to eat turnips and cabbages like the rest of us." She treated herself to a quart of maple syrup and arranged for him to pick up her mail in the nearest town.

He waited on her himself. No one else came in. She was aware of doors banging and voices calling in the back of the building, but there was no sign of his wife or his family.

"How's the bear?" he asked.

"Oh, fine, I guess," she said, not knowing what else to say. "It looks pretty miserable tied up that way."

"Don't forget, however human it looks, it's a wild critter after all. Don't get soft with it."

"Did they take it for walks?"

"I don't know what the hell they did with it, pardon my French."

"It could use a swim."

"I wouldn't fool around with it. You might have to get to know it the hard way. I guess it looks kind of little when it's all curled up in the shed, but a bear's a heavy animal. It can knock your head off with a wallop. I bet it weighs six hundred pound."

"Didn't Mrs. Leroy ever take it out?"

He grinned. "Oh, she was a funny one. I've seen her with that bear. She used to take one of them straight kitchen chairs out to the back yard and sit and just talk at it for hours. Maybe French talk, maybe Cree, I couldn't make it out. She's a wonderful knitter, Mrs. Leroy, and on a fine day she'll sit there and talk and knit a mile a minute. The two of them together, they were a sight to see." His eyes got shifty again. There was something he had thought of, but didn't want to say.

"It isn't vicious, is it?"

"That bear? Jeepers, no. It's just . . . well, he's just a plain old bear, and he's been on that chain for so many years there's no telling what would happen if you let him loose. He might kill you, he might just sit there, he might walk across the yard and take a leak. Mrs. Leroy wouldn't think very much of you if you let it get away, though, and neither would the farmers further back along the shore."

She promised she would not, and drove the motorboat home alone, back along the creeping river. The water was dark, yet clear and metallic-looking, too cold to trail a hand in. She steered between shoals and islands and reedy shores to her dock, and carried her groceries into the isolated house.

That evening, she went upstairs with a rag and polished glass inkwells and penracks and the yellowed globes. She fussed with the telescope until she could see far down the empty river in the last of the light. Then she lighted the Tilley lamp, put a roll of labels in her typewriter and began the imperious business of imposing numerical order on a structure devised internally and personally by a mind her numbers would teach her to discover.

At first she worked quickly, almost desperately. She had a presentiment of an unknown joy awaiting her, a feeling that it could easily be taken away. She must be virtuous and efficient. It was like the smell that scented the air morning and evening, elusive and mysterious. Everyone wants to be Robinson Crusoe and to be a half-hatched Robinson Crusoe is almost unbearable. If the experience is not to be taken away I must begin on it at once, she thought.

After an hour, she was shivering. She went downstairs, put on a pullover, put the kettle on. On her way to the outdoor toilet she could see the bear's night-green eyes following her. As she went through the yard to the back door he got up and grunted. She stood quite still, letting her eyes adjust to the dark so she could see his dark form. He lumbered gently forward, his head lower than his scruff, looking bashfully at her. When he reached the end of his chain, he sat down on his hams and grunted like a pig.

Picking her way over the dark rough boards of the woodshed, she went in and got him the scraps from her supper. He lapped them up at once, then looked at her it seemed, beseechingly. She stood as far back from him as she could, and held out a stiffened hand. He licked it with a long, ridged, curling tongue, but when she tried to pat his head he swung it sideways and away from her.

42

Upstairs again, she cruised the bookcases in the dim light, lovingly turning their square brass keys, gently easing out a volume here, a volume there. The collection was very fine, though it pointed to no scholarly proclivities, and it had been maintained by Cary's descendants so that it covered the nineteenth century in three languages. Hume. Smollett. Hume and Smollett. Byron, of course, and the other romantics. Sheridan, Dickens. Thackeray. Eliot. No Trollope. Mrs. Gaskell. Bulwer Lytton. Ah, Darwin — but not a first edition. Jane Austen, of course. De Maupassant. Lamartine. Goethe, Schiller, a lot more German, though she did not read German.

Those credits to womankind, Mrs. Hemans ('The boy stood on the burning deck . . .') and Eliza Cook ('I love it, I love it; and who shall dare/To chide me for loving that old arm-chair?'). Young's *Night Thoughts*. Oh, everything.

She had arrived in her trade because she loved reading. It struck her as she peered into the great bookcases how little reading she did now. Mostly she dealt with undecipherable papers and overwritten maps. As far as books went, she was concerned with their externals only. Here, she would have time to read.

She found one volume of the *Penny Cyclopaedia* produced by the Society for the Promotion of Useful Knowledge, under the chairmanship of Lord Brougham, lying on its side. She picked it up and a slip of paper floated to her feet.

In the Linnaean system, brown, beautifully curled, minute handwriting told her, *Ursus comes between Mustela and Didelphis. The order includes Arctos, the true bears; Meles, the badgers; Lotor, the raccoon; and*

43

Luscus, the wolverine. Walk: plantigrade; grinders: tuberculated; stature: large. Carnivorous. Frugivorous. Tail generally short. Brain and nervous system fairly developed. Claws for digging, non-retractable. Senses acute. Cylindrical bones more similar to man's than those of other quadrupeds, esp. the femur. Therefore able to rear up and dance. Tongue has a longitudinal groove.

Kidneys lobed as in bunches of grapes; no seminal vesicles. Bone in penis. In the female, the vagina is longitudinally ridged. Clitoris resides in a deep cavity.

Sparks showered from the cedar logs. She checked the handwriting against the samples in her files. It was indisputably Cary's. When the lamp began to fail she went to bed and dreamt of what she had read on the other side of the paper: saw the Kamchatkans on their high peninsula looking at her through the windows and snowmasks they make from the gut of the bear, and heard the whistle of mown grass falling where they slashed it with the sharpened shoulderblade of the bear.

VII

Morning in the city is to be endured only. There is no dawn any more than there is real darkness. There is only, after rainfall or street-sweeping, the sound of tires squealing on wet asphalt. Here, she woke shivering again and raised her nose to the air like an animal. The light in the bedroom was extraordinarily white. She pulled herself out of the Colonel's baronial bed and went to the window. The world was furred with late spring snow.

It was the soft, thick stuff that excites you unless you are driving or half dead, packing snow already falling in caterpillars off the greening branches. She sniffed again. Snow has its own cold smell. She put her boots on and went outside and peed in it, wondering how many years it was since she had yellowed snow. There was no sign of the bear. He had crawled into his byre to hibernate again.

She stood outside, listening. Small birds cheeped. The river sucked at reeds and stones. Branches cracked, rubbed against each other. Bird-feet rustled in dry leaves. Perhaps, too, that was the bear snuffling and snoring in his house.

She went inside, hating to disturb the precious felted silence. She filled the kettle, nervously scraping the dipper against the pail. She dressed and heard the tearing noises of her clothes. She stomped her shoes on and heard the laces whirring against each other as she tied them up. She scraped the butter knife against her toast. Stirred her coffee with a jangling spoon. Not everyone, she thought, is fit to live with silence.

The bear came out of his shed when she rattled his pan. Wearing the same cowed expression, he scooped his dish towards him with his paw. She held her hand out. He put his muzzle briefly in her palm. Then turned away to eat. Good. They were beginning to be friends.

She went upstairs to card and classify in the brilliant light. The Colonel's will specified that the books were not to be separated from the house. She and the Director had plotted to found a summer Institute, if the property was suitable. Now it looked to her as if the material he owned was all imported. The use of the building by scholars would only be justified if there was local history involved. You do not come to northern Ontario to study London in 1825.

Or do you? she wondered mischievously.

The snow continued to drop away from the branches, shooting across her sightlines as she worked. By noon it was gone. She put on her boots and went outside to explore.

The obvious thing about islands, which one tends to forget once one has landed on them, is that they are water-creatures. This one was small. Cary's clearing was bounded by almost impenetrable bush. There was no beach, and here the bush came right down to the shore. To the south of the house, however, a path had been cleared to the southern point, and there, in one of the Colonel's magnificent maples, a kind of crow's nest had been built. She climbed its wooden ladder and, shading her eyes with her hand like a cartoon sailor, saw far beyond the river's mouth to the open reaches of the inland sea.

She found a break in the brush, and entered the forest solemnly, as if she were trespassing in a foreign church. The ground was spongy, creeping and seething with half-born insects, still white here and there with the morning's snow. She made her way, convincing herself that on an island she could not get lost, to a rise in the land, climbed its littered slope, and found herself standing by a minute pond. Bubbles of marsh gas or beaver breath rose lazily from its black depths. She looked up and saw a pair of goshawks high in a dead tree, ill-wishing her. She went back to the house swinging her arms for exercise. She wished it were warm enough to swim.

She went upstairs to work. She was, after all, and however chilled, a reliable person. She sat down at her desk and proceeded to record what there was to record. Then, somehow, because she wondered how he would react to the snow, she began to think about the bear.

His bigness, or rather his ability to change the impression he gave of his size, excited her. Yesterday he stood there staring at me like a fur coat, she thought, and today he looked like some kind of raccoon. She went to the window to see what he looked like now and she heard a very odd kind of sound: a crooning or mourning. Yet from her aerie she could see nothing.

She went downstairs. Out the back door. There, on the stoop sat an old, old woman. She was babbling and crooning to the bear.

She was an old Indian woman. She looked like the woman who used to peddle bittersweet on the street when Lou was a kid, a toothless old Indian crone in many cardigans and running shoes, ten cents a bunch, and Lou bought it and her mother said it was a waste of money, a form of begging.

She was babbling to the bear, who lay half-in half-out of his shed watching her closely. One of his eyes winked once.

Lucy Leroy looked round, almost at once. "Allo," she said, holding out a withered hand, smiling with toothless gums. She was totally withered. Lou imagined the body under the old pinned clothes, imagined its creases and weatherings, the old thin dugs: I will be like that, she thought.

But the woman's eyes were alive as oysters. She held out her hand. "New lady," she said. "New lady. Good bear. Good bear."

"I didn't hear your boat."

Lucy grinned unnervingly, still holding onto her hand.

"Good bear," she said. "Good lady. Take care of bear."

"I don't think I really know how to take care of him," she said modestly citified.

Lucy's live eyes crinkled. "Good bear," she said. "Bear your friend. I was a young girl once. I came from Swift Current. Married a man, came here. Now I live on Neebish. He's a good bear. I am one hundred years old. I can read. I went to the mission school."

"And the bear?"

Lucy's face crinkled with some inconceivable merriment. She did not look one hundred years old, only eternal. "Shit with the bear," she said. "He like you, then. Morning, you shit, he shit. Bear lives by smell. He like you."

Lou restrained herself from shuddering and heard a motorboat. Lucy stood up. She came barely to Lou's breast. She was old and crooked. "That's Joe. I go."

Snap, crackle, she was off. The bear didn't move, and neither did Lou. She had no time to. Lucy was gone, that was all, a hundred years old, gleaming, toothless, and gone. A boat gunned off.

Lou squatted and looked at the bear. She thought of the outhouse with its frilled enamel lids. She thought of European toilets with footprints and holes. She looked at the bear and began to laugh. He looked as if he was laughing too.

VIII

The next morning when she went outside, the sun, as if to compensate for the aberration of the late snow, had real warmth to it. She stood for a moment and stretched in it. It raked her skin through her pyjamas. She thought for a moment, then gingerly tiptoed to the bear's cabin, hunkered by its wall, and with some difficulty moved her bowels meagrely. The bear, lying with his body inside, his head in the sun, moved its nostrils only.

"Come on," she said, when she was finished the humiliating act. "Come on." Tugged at his chain. Unhooked the chain from the post. At first he did not respond; then he got groggily to its feet. When she tugged hard, he padded after her. Hoping that he would not run and drag her fatally after him, she led him to the water.

He was nervous and passive. There was no tautness in the chain. She kicked off her boots, hitched up her pyjama bottoms and led him gingerly into the water. He sat down and wiggled his matted bottom against the stones. Then he moaned lightly, and put his head down to drink. Finished. Looked up at her for a signal. What should he do? She saw that her feet had turned blue and stepped out of the water behind him, onto the warm new grass. He strained and went forward, then changed his mind and came back to her.

To her this first small rebellion was a return of life, and she rejoiced in it. She let the chain loosen, without letting it go. He lowered himself again into the shallow water, and a great shudder made eddies around him. His short tail wagged out behind him. He edged himself further forward and slapped the water with his paws. She was afraid for a moment that he would pull away, but no, when he reached the end of his chain he backed up, relaxed, and sat with his back to her, sniffing the air around him. Impulsively, she scooped water with her hands and poured it over him. He shook and shuddered. She could have crowed.

Afterwards on the bank, he shook and wet her through. She laughed, let his chain go entirely and dashed to the house. Found an old brush in the woodshed, sat down and curried him. What a mother I am, she thought.

In the afternoon, another slip of paper fell out of another book:

Table of Longevity:
Platypus — 10 years
Chimpanzee — 40 years
Castor — 19 years

Marten — 15 years
Wolf — 16 1/2 years
Ursus Arctos — 34 years
Leo — 30 years
Elephas — 69 years

She looked at the note. Turned it over and over.
So he wrote little things down about bears. God help
him, he'd better have written little things down about
other things too, the selfish bastard. What the Institute needed was not a nice house, or a collection of
zoological *curiosa* but material to fill in the history of
settlement in the region. There was no research material at all for this township between the period of
Jesuit visitation and the resurvey of 1878, and here
was Cary sending her little notes about — bears. She
wanted to pick up each of his books and shake them
till the spines fell off. Instead, she carefully filed and
dated his note, marking its envelope with the name of
the book it fell from. Perhaps when she was very old
she would return and make a mystical acrostic out of
the dates and titles of these books and believe she had
found the elixir of life.

"Cary, you old wastrel," she found herself saying,
staring up at his portrait over the fireplace. From
behind dusty glass, the scarlet of his tunic faded to
pink, but his cheeks doll-rosy, the bridge of his nose
eroded by sunbeams, black eyes still flashing, the
lean, elegant colonel stared back at her.

When she turned to look out his window, she
thought his eyes followed her and for a moment she
was Cary advancing boldly on the new world, *Atala*
under one arm, *Oroonoko* and the handbooks of
Capability Brown under the other. Hastily, she fled to

the notes of his granddaughter. "Colonel John William Cary was both classically and militarily educated at the Royal Military College, Great Marlow, and continued his studious habits even when he was abroad. Thus he was well enough educated to converse knowledgeably with Byron at Malta. When he was stationed in what is now Italy he imported books at great expense from England. He was what is known as book-poor. His wife resented his passion."

I bet she did, Lou thought.

Ursus Arctos, ours, orso, Bär, Björn: inhabits the mountainous districts of the Alps, Pyrenees and Arctic Circle. Also, Siberia, the Kamchatkan Peninsula and North America. The Laplanders venerate it and call it the Dog of God. The Norwegians say, "The Bear has the strength of ten men and the sense of twelve." They never call it by its true name lest it ravage their crops. Rather, they refer to it as "Moedda-aigja, senem cum mastruca," the old man with the fur cloak.

She looked out the back window. "Greetings to my people," she said. Went on with her work.

The long holiday weekend came. Briefly, the inlet filled with motorboats, pennants of smoke arose from other little islands. She felt invaded, though no one stopped at her dock. One afternoon she sat out on the lawn in a deck-chair, pretending not to notice when fishermen waved. That night she saw sky-rockets over the water and thought she smelled a million roasting marshmallows. She pictured Cary unfolding a faded Union Jack on the Queen's Birthday. He would have thought Victoria an improvement on Queen, Queen Caroline but disapproved of the prudishness even then advancing on the bush.

She settled into a routine. She worked all morning, then in the afternoon disappeared into the bush to walk on carpets of trilliums and little yellow lilies; hepatica and bunchberries. The basswoods had put out huge leaves. Often, scarved and gloved against the black flies, she lingered by the beaver pond. The goshawks stared at her from their barkless elm with impenetrable eyes.

If the day was warm, she took the bear to the water. He showed no doggish enthusiasm when she went to get him, simply followed her docilely when she tugged his chain. Then, in the water, sat like near-sighted baby placidly enjoying the return to liquid existence.

Once a week Homer brought her mail. Once a week she shopped at Homer's, sometimes in the now long evening sleekly putting along the channel causing heron and bittern to rise from the reeds. Once she drove into a nearby town for whisky and fresh meat. The Government had opened a liquor store in an orange and white trailer.

She worked in the morning and in the evening, less efficiently than she would have in the office because for once she wanted to take her time.

One evening she took her supper out to eat on the woodshed stoop in the sun (the darkness of the kitchen seemed to indicate that whichever of the Carys had built the house had not consulted his woman). The bear sat as close to her as he could at the end of his chain. She unsnapped it and he came to sit by her knee. She reached out a hand and kneaded his scruff. His skin was loose on his back and his fur was thick, thick, thick, and beginning to gleam from the swimming. He stared at her earnestly, swinging his head from side to side, as if he could not see her with both eyes.

Later, she went upstairs again. She was deeply absorbed in the classification of a series of Victorian natural history manuals when she heard an unfamiliar sound downstairs and stiffened; froze; held her breath. A door squealed open.

For a moment, defenceless, she felt panic. Then, without knowing why, she relaxed a little. The heavy tread that advanced was accompanied by a kind of scratching: claws clacking on the kitchen linoleum.

She heard him slaking his thirst at the enamel water pail.

She went to the top of the stairs. She saw him below in the darkness staring up at her. "Go back to bed," she told him.

His thick legs pumped up the stairs towards her. She retreated to her desk and sat on it, hunching towards the window.

Inside the house, he looked very large indeed. At the top of the stairs he drew himself up to his full height, in that posture that leads the bear to be compared to the man, with his paws dangling: he's a cross between a king and a woodchuck, she thought as he moved his head short-sightedly around. Then he raised one hand in salutation or blessing, and folded himself down on all fours again. Deliberately he walked around the far end of the chimney wall and lay down in front of the fire.

He knows his way, she thought.

She went cautiously to him. He was wriggling like a dog, trying to get comfortable. "Well," she said to him, "you've got your nerve."

The room seemed darker now. She lit an extra lamp. The bear looked up when it hissed to a glow, then laid its head on its forepaws and appeared to go to sleep.

She discovered it was impossible to type with her back to him. She made nothing but mistakes. Therefore, she got herself a drink and a book and settled down on the sofa beside him, thinking of Homer's warning: "He's a wild animal, after all."

She had picked a life of Beau Brummell out of the bookcases. Perhaps the way to Cary was through his contemporaries, though she could no more imagine the Beau in the bush than he could perhaps have imagined himself dirty and insane among the nuns of Calais.

The book had all the worst characteristics of Post-Victorian biography. It was pompous and speculative, badly researched, unindexed. The world has improved in a way, she thought, and in her head a whirl of scholars whizzed from fact to fact, all of them weeding and verifying the life of the dandy who invented the necktie and became so obsessed with his pride he insulted the king. Cary might have known him, she thought. He was in London after the war ended. Perhaps he dined at White's with an officer friend. Would he have snubbed the man who refused to serve his country in Manchester, or would he have laughed and rubbed his gloves together? Maybe he took one look and decided to emigrate then and there.

The fire blazed. The bear slept wheezily, occasion-

ally winking his fireward eye. She grew warm, kicked
off her shoes, and found herself running her bare foot
over his thick, soft coat, exploring it with her toes,
finding it had depths and depths, layers and layers.

The Beau was dominating duchesses. The Beau
was on the make. How she disapproved of him, how
she admired him. His egg-like perfect sense of himself
never faltered. To circumstances and facts he never
bent. Lucky for him he never married, she thought: he
would have found domesticity squalid. Cornet Brummell who would not go to Manchester (not on liberal
grounds, refusing to quash a popular riot, but because
gentlemen do not go to Manchester), who would not
touch reality with a barge-pole, who invented the
necktie and made it fashionable to be clean....really!

She looked up at Cary and down at the bear and
was suddenly exquisitely happy. Worlds changed.
Two men in scarlet uniforms, two men who had lived
well; neither rich or highly well born, both she was
sure, in the end, ruined. She felt victorious over them;
she felt she was their inheritor: a woman rubbing her
foot in the thick black pelt of a bear was more than
they could have imagined. More, too, than a military
victory: splendour.

Nonsense. Too much whisky. She got up and blew
out the extra lamp. It was time to go to bed. Cary and
Brummell had no need of her pity or her victories.
Cary was not ruined: this was his house and she was
in it. Nonsense. What a fool she was.

"Come on," she said brusquely to the bear. She
put the screen in front of the fire and turn out the
Tilley lamp. The bear stood up and yawned, lum-

bered in front of her down the stairs, his hindquarters shifting awkwardly as he made the downward climb. He went out the back door without looking back, and she locked it. Pumped herself a clean pail of water. went to bed.

IX

The next morning she sat in the sun chewing her breakfast and shivering because the weather had taken a turn for the worse. The bear lay as usual in the doorway of his byre, staring at her. What does he think? she wondered.

She had read many books about animals as a child. Grown up on the merry mewlings of Beatrix Potter, A. A. Milne, and Thornton W. Burgess; passed on to Jack London, Thompson Seton or was it Seton Thompson, with the animal tracks in the margin? Grey Owl and Sir Charles Goddamn Roberts that her grandmother was so fond of. Wild ways and furtive feet had preoccupied that generation, and animals clothed in anthropomorphic uniforms of tyrants, heroes, sufferers, good little children, gossipy housewives. At one time it had seemed impossible that the world of parents and librarians had been inhabited by creatures other than animals and elves. The easy way out, perhaps, since Freud had discovered infantile sexuality.

Yet she had no feeling at all that either the writers or the purchasers of these books knew what animals were about. She had no idea what animals were about. They were creatures. They were not human. She supposed that their functions were defined by the size, shape and complications of their brains. She supposed that they led dim, flickering, inarticulate psychic lives as well.

He, she saw, lay in the weak sun with his head on his paws. This did not lead her to presume that he suffered or did not suffer. That he would like striped or spotted pyjamas. Or that he would ever write a book about humans clothed in ursomorphic thoughts. A bear is more an island than a man, she thought. To a human.

Last night: the horrifying slither of his claws on the linoleum; his change of stature at the top of the stairs. She had quailed, literally quailed: sunk back into the window nook. If she had been standing up, her knees would have knocked again. He was shorter than she was, not much over five feet tall, but immensely dense, deep in the chest, large-limbed. His outstretched arm was twice the girth of a man's.

Non-retractable claws, he has: she stared at the bear with respect and a residue of fear.

Old Lucy Leroy, now, what does she say to the bear?

How come he knows his way upstairs?

No, back to the beginning: how and what does he think?

The clank of her fork in her plate seemed to wake him from his reveries. He rose slowly and slouched towards her, moving his head in that snake fashion that seemed natural to him. She realized he was still unchained and stood up nervously, thinking, I don't want him to smell my fear. She took a step towards him and stroked his head. He licked her hand once and ambled back to his byre. She had no difficulty snapping his chain on the link of his collar.

Whatever he thinks, she decided, he behaves very well. And went upstairs to work.

She found last night's book on Beau Brummell on the sofa. It seemed crazy to want drag him into the history of this place, away from tea with the Duchess of Whosit who was so fond of dogs, from the clubs and banquets where he obtained supremacy by unmitigated gall. Yet this fine sloping lawn, its spread of magnificent trees along the riverbank, its carefully sited lantern view, were products of his place and time, for as much as Blake and Wordsworth, Cary and Brummell had wanted a better life. The egotistic child attempting to attract the attention of the sovereign at Eton, the high-coloured young officer on the thunderbox, map-dreaming in Malta, were as infected by romanticism as the poets they would have scorned as lower class. And look where their adventuring had led them.

She gave herself a tough morning of work. At noon, the skies opened up. It was raining as if it had never rained before. Raining buckets, raining thick sheets of grey water. Thunder rolled. The skies flashed lightning. The sky was dark grey. The wide river flattened and puckered to receive the raindrops. Mist began to rise. She could hear the lawns turning into mush.

She went to the back window and stared towards the den of the bear. His yard was a sea of mud, and dimly she saw his eyes gleaming in the darkness. I can't bring him in tonight, she thought.

Rain thrummed on the roof and cascaded off the eaves. She could not remember ever having seen such rain except in England. She wondered if there was a lightning rod on the lantern. It was a miracle it didn't leak.

The rain made her want to urinate. She went downstairs and found, as she had expected, a rose-painted, lidded chamber-pot in the bedside table. And used it gratefully. Resisted, then, the urge to crawl into her sleepingbag and put her hands over her ears. The bear, she thought affectionately, is in his sleepingbag with his hands over his ears. He has no middle-class pretensions, no front to keep up, even to himself. She went into the kitchen and began to make a pot of soup.

Late in the day, the rain stopped suddenly. The sun came out and gleamed through the trees, turning her view from the library into an astonishing tunnel of green. She put on her boots and went down to the river. The boat was half sunk. She would bail it later. Now she wanted to listen to the riverworld shaking the rain off its wings.

A bittern boomed eerily. With a rush, a flock of returning swallows careened across the sky. A fish leapt. At her feet, frog spawn winked in the sun.

X

The next morning was hot. She took the bear down to the river, hooked his chain on a nail in the dock, and jumped naked into the water beside him. He seemed enormous, with his fur alternately flaring out and clinging seal-like. She dog-paddled beside him, scooping little waves towards him. He slapped the water with his paw in return.

The water was icy. She was about to swim to shore, when playfully he swam under her, then, with a sudden turn, tried to leap over her. She sank underwater and opened her mouth to scream. She choked, and trying to rise to the surface, found him above her. For a moment she thought she had drowned; then she found air and courage to propel herself the few feet to the shore, where she threw herself on the soggy bank, rebelliously panting.

Then she felt the tremendous shower of his shaking beside her. A moment later, he began to run his long, ridged tongue up and down her wet back. It was a curious sensation.

Much later, she took herself upstairs to work, for there seemed no reason to lie about savouring fright. She was, however, shaken, and her sensation of narrow escape was not helped by the fact that it reminded her of a time when, in a fit of lonely desperation, she had picked up a man in the street. She still shied away from the memory of how he had turned out not to be a good man. Surely the bear . . . no: it was fright that linked them, fright and flight.

Book, book. Always, when these things happen, pick up a book. A paper floated out:

In Wales, the bear was used as a beast of chase. The name Pennarth means bear's head.

Item: My Lorde usith & accustomyth to gyfe yerly when his Lordshipe is at home to his barward when he comyth to my Lord in Cristmas with his Lordshippe's beestes, for makyinge of his Lordschip pastime, the said xij days, xx s.—Household book, the Earl of Northumberland.

The Esquimaux believe that the soul of a wounded polar bear tarries three days near the spot where it leaves his body. Many taboos and propitiatory ceremonies are observed with regard to the slaughtering of the carcase and the consumption of the flesh.

To the Lapps, the bear is King of the Beasts. Hunters who kill him must live three days alone, else they are considered unclean.

"But he wasn't chasing me, he was playing with me!" she cried aloud. The thought of the bear baited, flayed, pursued, was agony. "Oh Lord, keep him safe from harm!" she heard herself saying. She had not prayed in years.

XI

Homer came next day with his son, Sim, and a rototiller and seed. She had forgotten he had said he would help her start a garden.

To the north of the house there was a little path in the woods that led to a clearing full of fungus and poison ivy.

"Them raspberries there," he said. "You could cut back them raspberries. There's nothing like the raspberries here. Some say old Colonel Cary brought them. You don't get them down south like that. One thing about raspberries: they love wood ash. Sim'll cut them back for you — I can tell you're not much of a gardener, the way you just stand there — and by the middle of the summer you'll have some dandies. And you watch out around here in the summer, too: there's lots of wild asparagus. Little narrow stuff. Sparrow-grass, people call it. Whenever I find a bunch of wild asparagus I take off my hat and say a little thank-ee to Colonel Cary, because I know he brought that. Like mushrooms?" He stood staring at her, eyes gleaming, a strange salesman's smile on his face.

"Sure."

"Morels in the woods. May morels. Have you been in the woods back there?"

"Just the other way, to the beaver pond."

"Oh, it's all bog, there, but up here, you know he used to have an apple orchard. Now Sim and I'll get this part cleared up and tilled for you, and you just go back in there and look for morels. Ugly things they are, but they're good eating. Fry 'em in butter. Guess they're why I never got excited about margarine, so many things are tasty with a bit of butter or bacon fat don't work out with margarine. Now we'll get this coarse-dug for you and then you can fork it and if you're smart you won't be too much of a lady to snatch some manure out of the bear's stable — oh, I seen you, I know you can take him and tie him up the other side of the yard, you're getting to be great friends with that bear — and manure the plot with that. Chicken manure'd be better but beggars can't be choosers. Then about the end of the week you can put your seeds in. You'll lose some to the rabbits but you should be able to get up some beans and a few cabbages and peas. There're stakes in the shed.

"Your turnip and your potato — that's what the old folks used to live on — you won't be around here long enough to wait for them, I reckon."

The rest of what he had to say was drowned out by Sim at the rototiller, a machine that made more noise than a hundred motorboats. She fled into the bush and discovered black, gnarled old apple trees, and **dozens** of the strange decayed phalluses that are morels. She thought of cooking them up for Homer and the silent, albino-looking Sim, but suddenly their racket stopped, they waved good-bye and chugged off into the dusk.

She cooked and ate her morels and found them good — they tasted the way truffles were supposed to taste in books but never seemed to in reality — and went upstairs to spend the evening reading, drinking Scotch whisky and licking a Lifesaver sucker Homer had stuck in her bag of groceries and seeds as a treat. It was long after midnight when she went to bed, none the wiser from the perusal of a book that purported to reconcile Genesis and *The Origin of Species*.

XII

Now, the long warm days taught her the meaning of serendipity. She seeded the garden carefully, then on impulse took the bear to root in the morel patch, where he grubbed in a kind of ecstasy, digging and snuffing and once in a while raising his weak eyes to her, going back to work as if there might be no more time. Afterwards, she took him to the edge of the river, where he sat in the water like a large-hipped woman, dragging his bottom on the stones.

"I love you, bear," she said.

That night, the bear's heavy tread on the staircase did not disturb her. Let him come. She had taken down a book and was making a card for it. She had just shaken it gently; a slim slip of paper had fallen out. She was leaning over when she heard the bear on the stairs. Their eyes met around the chimney.

"Go sit down," she said, and he did.

St Ursula, Br., had 11 or 71 thousand virgins. See: Selder's note on the 8th song of Drayton's Polyolbion. The Ursuline order, founded at Paris in 1604 by Mme de Ste Beuve, was formed to succour the poor and educate the young. Ursula and her children populate the sky.

On the reverse side of the paper was a recipe for ink.

The bear sat by the fireplace. She raised her head and closed her eyes and thought of the other pieces of paper that had fluttered out of books. She thought of Homer saying, "They've always had a bear." She thought of Byron's mother, vainly scrambling for money to maintain Newstead Abbey and feed the bear. She looked at the bear. He sat there, solid as a sofa, domestic, a rug of a bear. She went to kneel beside him. He smelled better than he had before he started swimming, but his essential smell was still there, a scent of musk as shrill as the high, sweet note of a shepherd's flute.

His fur was so thick she could lose half a hand in it. She kneaded his hunched shoulders. It gave her a strange peace to sit beside him. It was as if the bear, like the books, knew generations of secrets; but he had no need to reveal them.

Methodically, because passion is not the medium of bibliography, she finished cataloguing the book she was working on. Made a small private mark on its card to indicate a bear-clipping had been found in it, started a new card, and marked on it on what page and in what book she had found the slip of paper. And, curiously, the time and date.

She spent the rest of the night making similar cards for the other slips of paper, though she could not assign accurate times and dates for the finding of them. She wondered, as she did it, why she was doing it; if she were trying to construct a kind of *I Ching* for herself. No: she did not believe in non-rational processes: she was a bibliographer, she told herself. She simply wanted the record to be accurate.

She went to bed at dawn, giving the bear his breakfast as she chained him in the yard. As soon as he got there, he crouched and made a great turd that steamed in the morning chill. She watched his face as his bowels moved, half-amused at herself to be looking for emotion, and there was none. She had nothing to contribute.

She slept until late afternoon, and in the evening, working alone upstairs without her friend, found a piece of paper which read, *Waldo, in the Ruthenian legend, a lost prince, is rescued from ignominy by a bear whose droppings are gold.* This she entered on another card.

The next morning, adjusted once more to normal time, she woke in high spirits. Lay for a moment enjoying the light. Went to the door to sample the sun. It was hot, but the island was suddenly steaming with black flies and mosquitoes. She retreated, slapping herself, and dressed.

Breakfasting loyally outside with the bear, she tried to remember how long the black flies lasted. She decided she had never known that. Mid-July, perhaps. She was trying to decide to regard the black flies as a good symptom of the liveliness of the North, a sign that nature will never capitulate, that man is red in tooth and claw but there is something that cannot be controlled by him, when a critter no larger than a fruitfly tore a hunk out of her shin through her trousers. Her leg streamed blood. She went inside.

In case the bear was disappointed (for she had discovered she could paint any face on him that she wanted, while his actual range of expression was a mystery), she went out, plastered with mosquito lotion, and took him down to the shallowest part of the channel, where the water was warm. There, while he swam on the end of his chain, always spluttering with surprise when he came to the end of his freedom, she sat with her legs under water, a hooded sweater on top, batting the insects away. The bear sat down on the brilliant stones and clawed and swatted as swarms of mosquitoes invaded his eyes and nostrils.

"Oh bear," she laughed. "We're a funny pair." He turned around and quite definitely grinned.

She struggled in the cloud of insects to get the garden going. The weather was damp, which was good for growth, but it disgusted her to wear her leather boots in the mud as she forked the furrows, knelt and weeded. She worked with a piece of cheesecloth tied around her head, felt like a colonial civil servant's wife in India, struggling to endure. The flimsy cloth tickled and swelled as she breathed. "Hey," she wanted to yell, "I'm a city feller." She went to bed bitten and blistered, with a new respect for farmers and pioneers.

In the middle of the night she heard his footsteps: thuds and gentle claw-scatterings on the kitchen floor. She lay still, not daring to breathe, thinking of the open bites on the back of her neck, remembering she had not fed him. She drew her sleepingbag around her neck, lay stiff and alarmed. He lumbered through the bedroom door and squatted by her for awhile, sniffing and snooping, his eyes faintly red in the dark. "What do you want?" she whispered, rigid with fear.

He sat for a long time staring at her, smelling at her. Then snuffled and sniffed and went back outside.

In the lore of Irelande, she read later (safe inside and the bear chained up, the windows closed against insects, insulated), *there was a god who was a bear. In the city of Berne in Switzerland, bears are kept in a pit, in remembrance of the heroic past of that city. Many good Christians there also honour those fine animals at the summer solstice, when creatures mate in full view of the populace. It is rumoured that even the pious pay them reverence in view of the ancient belief that they, not Adam and Eve, were our first ancestors.* This was folded into a copy of Hugh Miller's *The Testimony of the Rocks* presented to Colonel Cary by one A.N. Williamson, Cary's Island, 1859.

XIII

Now that the fishing season was going in earnest, she took the sound of motorboats in her stride, but this motor stopped, and she was startled. Peering out the window, she saw Homer tying up his silver fish. She ran downstairs, glad of human company.

"Hi, Homer."

"Saw ya had the bear in the river this morning."

"He gets miserable, just sitting there. And I wanted to get under the water, away from the flies."

"Just remember he's a wild critter." A reproof glinted on his glasses. She thought, I wonder what he'd say if he knew what happened last time? She had only taken him in this morning to conquer her fear.

"Did the Carys?" she asked.

"Well, I never heard anything from them about him at all. I brought you some beer. You been here a straight month, now. Figured we ought to celebrate. You're doing pretty well, you know."

It amused her to think she had passed some kind of test without knowing it. She wondered what she'd have had to do to fail.

"I could use a beer, Homer."

"I oughta fix up that old kerosene fridge out there in the shed, for you, but she's a bugger. How're you doing otherwise?"

They went into the kitchen. He decapitated two beers with his jack-knife. She told him she liked it fine here.

"Lot of people can't figure out how you stand it."

"What do you think, Homer?"

"Well, " said Homer, tipping back his head and his beer, "I think this is probably the plummiest job you've ever had, since your tastes run this way."

That pleased her. He was not one to underestimate his region, and his acceptance of her gave her a feeling she was not a tourist, not one to be scorned. It took the curse off his warnings about the bear. She felt comfortable with him at last.

Homer tilted his chair back against the kitchen wall and began to talk about the last Colonel Cary, the one who had left the island to the Institute. Who was a woman.

"It was like this," he said. "It was in the will that the estate had to go to the child who became a colonel. Well, one of the boys made it in the first generation because you could buy a commission and the old man had some money put away for it, and there were a lot of wars on then, and I guess he didn't do too badly; but one thing, he didn't get around to marrying very young. He was a good fifty, and the wife he brought back here was no spring either. So when they had their first child and it was a daughter, they got the minister down from the Falls in a hurry and christened her — Colonel.

"There was hell to pay for that four years ago when she died and left the place to your Institute, but she was a fine woman. Tough as nails and not bad-looking either. They sent her down to Montreal to be educated, and after that she taught in some girls' school or other for a while. Then when her mother died, she came up here to look after her Pa. He lived on til the 'thirties — we live a long time up here, it's darned healthy, and he must have been near a hundred — and then she went back to schoolteaching until she retired.

"There were a lot of relatives, but not many living around here. The old Colonel's wife wouldn't come up here, you know; Toronto was as far from England as she'd go. Two of the boys came up, and one of them had a logging business near the Sault, eventually. There was a daughter called Sarah Snowdrop who kep' house for him a while, but she was apparently worse than nobody and she had fits. Mostly he lived alone out back there in the log house. Once he got a gang of men together and built a sawmill over there on the other side of the river, but the river ain't as big as it looks and they had to dam it up three days to keep the wheel going two.

"Eventually, the wife in Toronto died and he went to the Falls and courted one of the Lazare girls. 'I've got an island and a house to myself,' he says, 'and a pianola, and Sarah Snowdrop can't keep house worth a damn.' 'You call that a house you're living in?' she asked him. 'I call it a hut. You build me a house on that godforsaken island of yours, and I'll take you serious even if you are a Protestant.'

"Margaret Morris, who's married to the foreman at the lumber mill in the Falls, she's got this all written down because her grandmother was Emily Lazare.

"Well, it was Katie Lazare he built this house for. They say it took him five years to get it together. Everything except the timber had to come by sail up the lake. Then just before it was finished, Katie died. Fever, pneumonia, Lord knows what.

"So then he went courting Emily, Margaret says. She was a wonderful woman, that Emily. She was dark, and some figured she had Indian blood in her, but the French are dark and you notice a lot of Scots and Irish women with eyes that black too. She could size a man up and cut him out a blue flannel shirt — and it was real flannel in those days, not that pyjama stuff — she make them double-breasted with two rows of buttons, like a uniform — without a scrap left over and it fit like a glove. She couldn't knit, but she got the Indians to knit for her, she couldn't read nor write, but she knew everything else. She was one of those women who kept the country up here going. She could cook and cut kindling and keep her kids alive and healthy. She married one of the Cadottes and had thirteen kids. No way she was going to marry an Englishman who was already old.

"After that they say he went kind of crazy, living alone here with his books. He had a bear he used to talk to. He got a bit better when his son and his wife came up to live with him. Times were still hard, then, but civilization was creeping in. The second Colonel's wife got the place organized a bit better and brought her furniture over from England. All those fancy tables belonged to her. When he died the hard winter of '78 this part of the north was already opened up. It wasn't a wilderness any more.

"His children used to come up here and visit him, mind you. They were a moneyed outfit, pretty well bred. They were used to an education in that family and they turned out a lot of doctors and lawyers. While Colonel Jocelyn was alive a lot of them would come up here in the summer and run around in their Chris Crafts.

"They were mad when she left it all to the Institute. She got on well with her cousins from Cleveland, but they were pretty well fixed. I figure she was right to leave it as a historic monument. It was a historic monument, damnit. Who else but Colonel Cary could have thrown away a fortune building a barn of a place like this anyway? The damn island's only a sandbar, you can't farm it. You can't put cottages on it now you have to have running water and septic tanks because of the pollution. All the summer people now want flush toilets and washing machines. Your shithouse, pardon me, was good ecology, as they say."

"Was she a tall woman, Colonel Cary?"

"Not tall, not short. Some taller than you, not much. She walked English style, as if she was riding a horse. She was the first woman to wear pants up here. Would've created a scandal if anybody had time for one. There were those who said she was a snob, and those in the family didn't get on with her. When they came to visit, she gave them a lot of things, china, silver. She said she'd no use for finery, all she wanted was her island.

"Fine woman, though. It was before we had snow machines but if she wanted anything in the winter she'd come over to our place pulling her little sledge. She was one person I never had any fear would fall through the ice.

"She lived mostly alone after she came back up here. I used to check on her every so often, though I hate walking on ice. Some people don't mind it, but me, I'm not brave that way. I don't trust ice. Known too many men gone through.

"The Leroys and the Kings were pretty good to her. She was friends of theirs. She and Lucy got along like a house on fire. You know, people will tell you Lucy's Métis, but that was a long time back. I figure she and Joe are nearly full-blooded Indians, and what that means is, you never know where they are.

"Now, she liked the odd beer too. Used to sit on the dock with me there after the flies had gone and we'd knock off a six-pack. She was a great gardener, and a great fisherman. She had big hands like a man, way bigger'n mine, and she didn't fool around with any lotions. Kept her house spick and span, and all the silver polished that she hadn't given away. Baked bread. Did all those things women are supposed to do and she kept herself with a trap line. There wasn't a lot of money by then in that family, you know, in spite of their being English gentry originally, and what there was got spent on this house, and on the original family in Toronto. She didn't have much of a pension. I guess now she could have sold all her furniture as antiques, but the antique business is pretty new. No, until she was an old woman she'd put on her waist-waders and shove off in the boat in the season and trap rat and beaver. That's tough, cold work, you got to be part Indian to put up with it, but she did it. She knew all the cricks and the inlets, she had a licence of course, and she wasn't afraid of the work. Yet when the Anglican missionary and his wife came through she set out the blue plates and what was left of the silver (when my wife saw the tea service her eyes popped out) and put on a dress like something out of an old Hollywood movie and make them feel like common clay.

"She got a lynx once, year before she died, when she was an old, old woman. I didn't ask her how or why. Suppose it was caught in one of the traps. All I know was she asked me to mention it to so-and-so because she didn't have a licence to trap it. She had to tan it and stretch it and hide it, couldn't show it to the regular dealer. There's a man from Quebec, somewhere up near the Saguenay, come round the odd time to pick up anything unusual: protected species, accidents (I mean, you get a lynx by accident, what're you going to do? Confess? Bury it? Not on your life.) and he gave her two hundred dollars I think she needed pretty bad.

"I saw that skin. It was a beauty. Not a hole in it. I don't know if it died in the trap or she strangled it. She could have. She was that fierce. She'd stretched it on willow and it was yellow and soft as a kitten."

"Was that her bear?"

"Nope. I don't know who gave her that bear, but you couldn't say it was hers. I never did, did I? She never liked that bear. Maybe Lucy gave it to her, but you couldn't say it was hers because she paid no attention to it. She seemed to think there's always been a bear out there, so I'll keep a bear. But I always felt sorry for it because Lucy and Joe were the only ones who paid any mind to it. The Colonel just sort of tolerated it. The one she was fond of was her Irish setter.

"Now that other bear she had before, he was a character. Followed her round the house like a dog. The hunters — you know, there's hunters and hunters, I haven't got anything against a man hunting for meat, I go north every year for moose and a moose licence isn't cheap. How'd you like to paddle that old cedar strip canoe twenty miles with half a ton of raw, dead moose in it? But hunting for moosemeat ain't the same as some dumb hunter coming along with a rifle with cross sights thinking he's Ernest Hemingway and shooting her bear through the heart when all he's doing is sunning himself on the dock."

She felt herself falling over with a little thud. Then remembered that the Colonel was not Lady Caroline Lamb, but a tough, boney old woman hooping the pelt of an illegal lynx to a willow wand.

"She was a great lady," she faltered.

"Nah," said Homer, scratching his head. "She wasn't a great lady. She was an imitation man, but a damned good one."

XIV

She was given to crises of faith. That evening, after
Homer left, she sat up in Colonel Cary's admirable
study, surely one of the great rooms of the world in
terms of adaptation to purpose, unable to read or to
settle to cataloguing. She wondered by what right she
was there, and why she did what she did for a living.
And who she was.

Usually these quandaries arose weeks after the
beginning of an absorbing assignment, but this one
had set in early, just after she had established her
working patterns. She understood technically and
even emotionally the need to redefine objectives, but
she could not understand why the period of redefini-
tion had to be accompanied by depression, an existen-
tial screaming inside herself, and a raucous interior
voice that questioned not the project she was working
on, but her own self. "What am I doing here?" she

would ask herself, and the interior voice would echo, "Who the hell do you think you are, having the nerve to be here?"

She had been drinking beer. Her head ached and spun. She also felt guilty, as if she had revealed to Homer some secret which was not hers to reveal. As if she had done something bad, and he knew.

She tried to concentrate on externals, on her cards, on her notes. She looked around at the bookshelves and realized that in order to make the job last the summer she would have to cheat. There wasn't an efficient week's work left. She could go soon; she did not want to go.

She always attempted to be orderly, to catalogue her thoughts and feelings, so that when the awful, anarchic inner voice caught her out, her mind was stocked with efficacious replies. "What am I doing here?" could be answered with lists. She had another stock of replies to "Who the hell do you think you are, attempting to be alive?" She justified herself by saying that she was of service, that she ordered fragments of other lives.

Here, however, she could not justify herself. What was the use of all these cards and details and orderings? In the beginning they had seemed beautiful, capable of making an order of their own, capable of being in the end filed and sorted so that she could find a structure, plumb a secret. Now, they filled her with guilt; she felt there would never, ever, be anything as revealing and vivid as Homer's story, or as relevant. They were a heresy against the real truth.

You could take any life and shuffle it on cards, she thought bitterly, lay it out in a pyramid solitaire, and it would have a kind of meaning; but you could never make a file card that said, "Campbell, Homer" convey any of the meaning that Homer had conveyed tonight. She would soon have to admit that up here she was term-serving, putting in time until she died. Colonel Cary was surely one of the great irrelevancies of Canadian history and she was another. Neither of them was connected to anything.

She felt childish, sulky. She knew she must do something specific until the mood passed off. It was no good to sit and brood. She went downstairs and untied the bear. Took him swimming, trying to enjoy his gorgeous rolls and splashings. But he, too, seemed subdued and full of grief. The shallow river channel was warm, but to get out to any depth she had to swim in water that was icy. For one short moment she laughed as the bear came floating to her with all but his eyes and nostrils submerged like a crocodile, but something clouded that too, and she took him to the shore in gloomy silence.

She went upstairs again and went through the cards she had made. The library was conventional, and the personal information about Cary was meagre. It was too early in her research to give them any meaning, and perhaps they would never have any meaning. She felt like some French novelist who, having discarded plot and character, was left to build an abstract structure, and was too tradition-bound to do so. She felt weak, unable to free herself from the concrete. She flew into distemper when she tried to fly into ideas.

Surely, surely, a practical voice inside her spoke up, that is not the point of the exercise at all: you are here simply to carry out the instructions of the Director.

Deep in her files was buried the original letter from the Director, instructing her to (a) catalogue the library left to the Institute by Colonel Cary on Cary Island, (b) make separate annotations regarding the history and condition of this library, (c) report at length on the suitability of Cary Island as a centre for research into the human geography of the northern region, and (d) list, with sources, any addition information that would be useful to historians interested in the Cary period of settlement.

She read the instructions twice and sighed with relief. Anything she did would be relevant. Now she had her licence to exist.

XV

Next morning, using a crude chart she made for herself by comparing survey maps and marine charts, she set out with the bear on his chain to explore. After a few minutes of his pulling on his chain, she let him go. He would come back, she knew.

She marked the dock, the outbuildings and the tree lookout. She marked a row of stones that appeared to have been a foundation. Then, winding a scarf tight around her head against the blackflies, she set off into the southern part of the bush where the bear had gone. She found him digging happily under a rotten log, filling his craw with mittfuls of earth and grubs. She stood for a moment listening to the eerie half-silence of the bush. The warblers were back. A woodpecker tapped. There was a motorboat far away.

The woods had lost the first innocence of spring. The skunk cabbage had unfolded in sheets, the trilliums were drying. The sun shone through thin foliage. She whistled to the bear and went on walking, beating a path parallel to the lapping sound of the shore, looking for stone formations, rotted cabin-shapes, anything, trying to think what it might have been like to arrive from Portland or Bath and find this.

In those terms, the island was unpretentious. She had seen parts of Canada that would cause any explorer to roll back his eyes like Stout Cortez. In spite of the river's beauty, and the probable violence of the colours in the fall, this was domestic.

Suddenly, she burst through the trees and found herself at the southern point, and thought, my God, how wrong.

The river was broad and turbulent. Islands and range-lights winked in the sun. The bear crashed through the bracken and bounded to her, snorting.

They came for this, she thought: they were landscape nuts. They intended to make watercolours and have Robert Adam do their drawingrooms, Humphry Repton their facades and Capability Brown their gardens. Failing that, they built log-cabins with handsomely proportioned windows, and not where the view was, but where the bog gave over to maple and sand and there was some protection from the weather. If their consols prospered, they replaced the cabins with tall Victorian houses and sent their sons out for gentlemen who could return in later summers for the view.

The ones who were most truly romantic perished horribly, she remembered. Fell through the ice, contracted pneumonia or tuberculosis, died of strange fevers, scurvy, depression, or neglect. Only the hardiest survived and there few memoirs. Often the diaries that were left to the Institute broke off when the settlers arrived from England. If you were building your own cabin, making your own cloth and soap and candles, furniture and tools, there was no time to concoct a bottle of ink or find a quill to use it with.

She was descended from a man who came over from the north of Ireland with a wife and ten children to join his brother in Ontario, who had nine children himself. In New York, when they were making their arrangements for the second stage of the journey, the eldest son went out to explore and disappeared. They hunted five days for him, had to leave without him, cried all the way to Canada. When they arrived months later at the brother's, he said, "But where's our Andrew?" whereupon the paterfamilias went upstairs and lay down and died. Leaving his brother with two women and eighteen children. There was a certain mad toughness and a definite fear of New York in the family still.

Cary would be what was called gentry, though, she thought. Not like our lot. A wife too grand to follow her man to the woods wasn't our sort of thing. We would have stayed with him to make sure he didn't take a drink.

Slowly, trying to keep from wetting her leather boots, she made her way, the bear behind her, around the magnificent point to the other side of the island, where Lucy Leroy was supposed to have a cabin. In the distance, bell-buoys tolled and lakers hooted, but as she circumambulated the whole island she found no sign of another habitation.

When she got home, she was exhausted. She had walked so little in the past month, her legs were atrophying. She went inside and lay down for a sleep.

When she awoke, it was dark. She struggled groggily with the lamps, made coffee, and went out to feed the bear. His eyes gleamed red-gold in the dark as he bustled towards his dish.

As she was finishing her supper, she heard him scratching to be let in and thought, why not? It struck her when she opened the door to him that she always expected it to be someone else. She wondered if he, like herself, visualized transformations, waking every morning expecting to be a prince, disappointed still to be a bear. She doubted that.

You say you will work, you work. She went upstairs to work. She always held herself to her commitments. In another incarnation she had worked on a newspaper among people who were always going to leave to write books, but meanwhile scurried from deadline to deadline, for missing a deadline was their form of Original Sin. She left the newspaper not to write but because when she was required to interview a baker on his fiftieth wedding anniversary she found him quailing lest she reveal the fact he had married his deceased wife's sister. That gave her a perverse desire, which she suppressed, to reveal his truth, and a vivid memory of courses in Victorian history. Suddenly her life on the newspaper seemed ephemeral and impoverished (and it is true that Greek newspapers, like certain insects, are called 'ephemerídes'), and she changed her life in order to find a place for herself in the least parasitic of the narrative historical occupations.

She went upstairs to work. The bear took some time to follow her. She was at her desk when he stood full height at the top of the stairs, she paid no attention to him. She had found an autographed first edition of Major Richardson's *Wacousta,* inscribed to John Cary with regards in 1832. She wished she had saleroom catalogues to ascertain its value. Meanwhile, she catalogued it and held it a long time in her hands. It was a rare, rare bird, worth coming here for.

There were other valuable books, Boston editions that were in fact pirated Canadian editions, produced without revenue to English and French authors, but nothing, so far, to equal *Wacousta.* Strange I have never read it, she thought, but I won't read this copy. Get myself a reading copy from Toronto and compare the texts. Well, Cary, you were somebody after all if you knew Richardson.

"Lie down, by duck, my beau," she said, for the find had put her in good humour. Then she reached for the next book, shook it for notes, and opened it. Trelawny's remembrances of Byron and Shelley.

She opened it and began to read (for it was not a sacred copy, not a rarity, it was dated London, 1932). Trelawny? The man who burned Shelley's body and saved the heart. Yes, that Trelawny. The pirate. Giant of a man. Went to Greece with Byron after Shelley died.

She began to read, enthralled. She had never read this book before, though the subject interested her. Why? Someone, some scholar, had told her it was a pile of rubbish. Most autobiography is rubbish, she thought. People remember things all wrong. But what amusing rubbish this is! What a man! Big. Abusive.

A giant. A real descendant of the real Trelawny, the one about the twenty thousand Cornishmen. Oh, I'll believe he's a liar.

Look at the bear, dozing and drowsing there, thinking his own thoughts. Like a dog, like a groundhog, like a man: big.

Trelawny's good. He speaks in his own voice. He is unfair, but HE SPEAKS IN HIS OWN VOICE.

She sat up and said that out loud. The bear grunted. She got down on her knees beside him. Colonel Cary had left her tiny, painful, creepily paper-saving notes. She was still searching the house to find his voice. She had an awed feeling that Trelawny and the bear were speaking in Cary's voice. Trelawny wanted to find a poet, to know a poet, because he couldn't be one, and he was romantic about poets. He lived to be old, he knew Swinburne and the pre-Raphaelites. There's some connection there.

Cary wanted an island.

She was excited. She wanted to know how and who this Cary was. Trelawny. Colonel Cary. The bear. There was some connection, some unfingerable intimacy among them, some tie between longing and desire and the achievable.

She lay beside the bear and read more Trelawny. Appalling blowhard, savage to both Byron and Mary Shelley. Byron was too sedentary. Shelley couldn't swim. He bought the boat for Shelley. It wasn't a good one.

She read about the drowning. Then she skipped to the end of the book. Oh Christ, he turned the shroud back to have a look at Byron's lame foot. Disgusting man.

All the Victorians, early or late, she thought, were morbid geniuses. Cary was one of them and bought himself an island here. He didn't have Ackerman's Views or Bartlett's prints to go by. He sensed what he wanted and came and found it.

How did he start wanting it? Did he come entranced by the novels of Mrs. Aphra Behn, then move on to *Atala* and the idea of the noble savage, then James Fenimore Cooper?

He came for some big dream. He knew it was going to be hard. There were no servants who would come to the remoter islands. Books were procured with the utmost difficulty, and the tale of their difficult acquisition had probably caused this library to be left to the Institute. But in return for the sacrifice of civilization as he knew it, what did Cary obtain? An island kingdom, safely hedged by books? The dissipation of the sound of revelry forever? Relief from white neckcloths? Or was it simply hope and change?

He came, she thought, to find his dream, leaving his practical wife behind him in York. He was adventurous, big-spirited, romantic. There was room for him in the woods.

"Bear," she said, rubbing her foot in his fur, suddenly lonely. The fire was too hot, and the fur rug had edged towards her. Oh, she was lonely, inconsolably lonely; it was years since she had had human contact. She had always been bad at finding it. It was as if men knew that her soul was gangrenous. Ideas were all very well, and she could hide in her work, forgetting for a while the real meaning of the Institute, where the Director fucked her weekly on her desk while both of them pretended they were shocking the Government and she knew in her heart that what he wanted was not her waning flesh but elegant eighteenth-century keyholes, of which there is a shortage in Ontario.

She had allowed the procedure to continue because it was her only human contact, but it horrified her to think of it. There was no care in the act, only habit and convenience. It had become something she was doing to herself.

"Oh bear," she said, rubbing his neck. She got up and took her clothes off because she was hot. She lay down on the far side of the bear, away from the fire, and a little away from him and began in her desolation to make love to herself.

The bear roused himself from his somnolence, shifted and turned. He put out his moley tongue. It was fat, and, as the Cyclopaedia says, vertically ridged. He began to lick her.

A fat, freckled, pink and black tongue. It licked. It rasped, to a degree. It probed. It felt very warm and good and strange. What the hell did Byron do with his bear? she wondered.

He licked. He probed. She might have been a flea he was searching for. He licked her nipples stiff and scoured her navel. With little nickerings she moved him south.

She swung her hips and make it easy for him.

"Bear, bear," she whispered, playing with his ears. The tongue that was muscular but also capable of lengthening itself like an eel found all her secret places. And like no human being she had ever known it persevered in her pleasure. When she came, she whimpered, and the bear licked away her tears.

XVI

She woke in the morning. The weather was like silk on
her skin. Wisps of guilt trailed around the edges of her
consciousness. She felt as if she had neglected something. What didn't I do?

Oh dear, what did I do?

I was reading Trelawny, getting high on Trelawny, feeling I knew Cary, feeling I had tracked down
the mentality, then I . . . the bear.

Sweet Jesus, what a strange thing to do. To have
done. To have done to one.

She tested herself, pinching her conscience here
and there to see if she felt evil. She felt loved.

It was a beautiful day. She went gingerly outside
in her nightdress. She was a little sore. She watered
the bear and scratched his ears and fed him. Then, for
her sins, went to the garden and worked for an hour,
painfully weeding. The rabbits were wrecking it, and

the lettuce was sour. She ought to have a fence or a .22, or just leave it alone.

I need meat, she thought.

She dressed, and without making breakfast she untied the motorboat and slid through the brilliant morning channel to Homer's. The world was enveloped in a kind of early summer bliss. Kingfishers splashed, fish leapt, lily pads spread out from the sides of the channel. Keats, she thought. Then, were the romantic poets the only people who saw?

On this kind of morning, yes. The weather demanded lyricism. The motor made awful gutterals against the crying of water birds. She felt curiously peaceful.

At Homer's there was a letter from the Director, demanding to know when she was coming back.

She bought a pad of paper and an envelope, and went outside; sat at one of Homer's picnic tables beside the river, and wrote, "Dear Director." Sucked her pen, started another page. "Dear David." No, "Dear Dr. Dickson" would do it. "I have been utterly absorbed in the Cary collection. It is, on the whole, better that we could have hoped, though rather orthodox as a nineteenth-century collection goes. I have found an early edition of *Wacousta* among some far more ordinary looking books, and hope to make other discoveries. There is also hope that journals will eventually turn up — but not a great hope, I confess.

"I have been working at a slower rate than usual because I have been forced to put in a garden in order to avoid scurvy. It would be as well if I were a fisherman too, but for messing about with boats I have no patience.

"There is a Molesworth map in good condition.

"If you wish me to do this job thoroughly and well you will have to allow me to spend the rest of the summer here. I am sure you will have no objection to my spending my annual leave at Pennarth." Scrawling her name, folding the paper clumsily, licking the envelope and entrapping a gnat, thumping it shut. The bugger misses me.

Her second letter was from a feminist friend enquiring why she was not doing research on a female pioneer for International Women's Year. She replied on a postcard of a bearcub halfway up a tree that she was having a wonderful time.

"There," she said, handing them to Homer. "Any meat today?"

"Nothing fresh. Doing any fishing?"

"No, I don't know how."

"There oughta be some good rods there. The Colonel did a lot of it. Just dig up some worms in your garden there and go out in the boat at dusk. It's peaceful, and the pike are good in that little cove across the river from you, behind the eastward shoal. Pike are good eating."

She shuddered, bought a dozen eggs, and left. She was an inland person, after all.

Still, when dusk came, the river looked appetizing, and there were thoughts she wanted to avoid. She got worms and found an old cork-handled fishingrod in the front hall, set out down the channel.

The mosquitoes were maddening. Once she had dropped her line in, she could hardly sit still. There were fish; she could hear them plopping, but she did not know that she wanted to catch them. Pike. Were pike really good eating? What was French for pike?

Brochet, Quenelles de brochet. Gelatinous and heavy, like gefilte fish. No thank you.

She went to pull in her line and leave and found, to her surprise, that there was a fish on it. As easy as that, was it? She tried to reel it in, but the reel tangled, only wanted to spin out backwards. It was an old cotton line as thick as string so she began, incautiously, to pull it in hand over hand. It cut her palms as the fish struggled away. She became determined. In spite of her diffidence, she now wanted the fish. She would kill it and eat it. She leaned out, nearly capsizing, and pulled and pulled.

Eventually and ungallantly, she landed it by hand. It was huge and yellowish. It had a long, evil-looking snout. It flopped over her feet in the bottom of the boat.

Using the line, which was surely beyond repair now, she tied it to an oarlock.

When she got back to the house, she had to get a knife to cut it away from the gunnels of the boat. Then run up again to find a net to carry the fish in. There was no net. She came back with a plastic shopping bag.

She cut the line, put her thumbs under the fish's gills, and flopped it into the bag. Not before she had gashed a finger on its spiny fins.

Now I'll have to cook it and clean it, she thought. Fish. Friday. In horrible white sauce with slices of hardboiled egg and spinach on the side. No. The only good fish is what your father made on camping trips.

Does it have the kind of scales you have to trim off backwards? she wondered. Do you skin and fillet it? Is there a knife sharp enough? Cripes.

It was a big fish, the kind real fishermen were proud of. She was already disgusted with it. It kept bumping against her in the shopping bag. "Good eating," she kept hearing Homer saying.

She put it on the kitchen counter. Plop. It eeled out of the bag into the sink, lay there panting for water. She felt she had done a frightful thing, removing it from its kingdom. Its mouth was all torn from the hook. How did she know it wasn't a rare gar-pike of Lake Michigan, strayed a hundred miles to thrill Louis Agassiz? Or full of mercury? She might get Minamata disease and be arrested for a drunken Indian. It had a sour and saturnine face. She could not love it.

Grinning ruefully, she recalled who would. She put it back in the shopping bag and lugged it out to the bear.

Tomorrow, she thought, dining in state on a bologna sandwich, Homer will ask me if I caught anything. I'll tell him I snagged the line.

She lit the lamps and went upstairs. She had left the office in disarray last night. She tidied, finished carding the shelf of books she had assigned herself, then settled down to read Trelawny properly. She had been too excited last night when his personality emerged and she confused him with Cary.

Still, he was pretty good. He noticed things. Didn't like Mary Shelley, or any woman, much. Useful articles, women, she could hear him thinking, when they keep to their place. She thought of the women the officers brought to Canada with them: beached, bent, practical, enduring, exiled. Still, as many there must have been who enjoyed tugging a new world out of the universe as cried and died.

Her fishy friend came up the stairs. His tongue bent vertically and he put it up her cunt. A note fell out of the book: *The offspring of a woman and a bear is a hero, with the strength of a bear and the cleverness of a man. — Old Finnish legend.*

She cried with joy.

XVII

Summer came in swiftly. Rabbits continued to worry the garden. The Director gave her his gracious permission to spend her holidays there, even threatened to come and visit her. She knew he would never leave the city.

Over the first of July weekend, the motorboats, the tourists, the water-skiers and the cottagers arrived: pallid but hearty summer people. At night, knowing they were still out on the river, she pulled down the blinds, and during the days she felt violated, for the sweet silence was gone. A family even came to the door and asked if she could show them her house. She declined the honour.

Lovers built bonfires on her beaches. Water-skiers leapt by her, waving. She did not feel friendly. She wanted to be alone with the bear.

The Laplanders venerate it, and call it the Dog of God. The Norwegians say, "The bear has the strength of ten men, and the sense of twelve." They never, however, call it by its true name, lest it ravage their crops or flocks. Rather, they refer to is as "Moedda aigja," the old man with a fur cloak.

Not that she neglected her work. She worked. Always, they had said of her, she was nothing if not conscientious. She had to work. And there was still enough to do. Aside from mere cataloguing, there was the inventory of the house to be made. (And each of its angled rooms seemed to contain innumerable little Victorian tables of a kind that distressed her: four-legged, small topped, of a height and size only for a Bible or a fern or perhaps one of those glass bells that displayed decaying birds or funeral wreaths. The splay of the table legs disgusted her.) There were many things to be counted, and with any luck there would also be things to be edited. For although the lawyer's inventory existed, it was not nearly complete.

One bright morning she woke in good spirits and disclosed to herself the fact that she had not even attempted to open the door to the basement. She was afraid of damp, spidery places. She breakfasted and briskly looked after the bear (they could not go swimming because there were four motorboats placidly fishing the channel) and, armed with two flashlights and an oil lamp, went through the door, downwards.

The nether region was indeed dark and spidery. To her relief, however, she found four filled oil lamps hanging in brackets from the beams. She lit them one by one and the basement flared into eerie dimensions.

Assisted by one of the flashlights, she began to explore. It interested her to find that on two sides the foundations of the octagon had been quarried further to form what presumably were cold-rooms, for one contained wooden racks and green-topped jarred preserves, and three totally withered apples. The other was empty save for the long-decayed form of a burrowing anima!.

Orderly people, the Carys. Here were stacked neat coils of stove-wire, ordered rows of pipe. Another corner formed a repository for wicker summer chairs. More discarded fern tables. Pictures (*The Soul's Awakening. Wolfe at Quebec,* but not, alas, the *Siege of Derry,* the one she had always wanted) with melted gilt and plaster frames. So they were not so sophisticated they missed the oleograph era.

Old, tasselled snowshoes with turned-up toes. A broken banjo. (Did they sing "Old Black Joe" on the porch steps at night?)

Then, along another wall, trunks; in fact, a history of trunks: hoop-topped ones with stamped tin bindings, doubtless lined with printed birds; large theatrical wicker hampers; wood-bound World War One footlockers; turn-of-the-century wardrobe trunks, fit to contain a hundred brides. Trunks upon trunks. Work. Treasure.

She grinned and took the boat down to Homer's and asked if he and Sim could lend her a hand.

"Want to get some stuff up from the basement," she said vaguely. Homer's eyes glinted behind his glasses. He went to the house part behind the store and spoke to his wife. Her voice rose high and pettish behind the rows of canned goods.

"Hepped on those damned Carys," Lou heard. "Open til nine and then goodness knows what time. Something queer goin' on, I betcha."

Lou blushed, felt like running away. She thinks I'm after him, she thought.

"You wife can come too," she said to Homer.

"The way she's carrying on, she might like to get her face wiped off," Homer said, without changing his cheerful grin. "She don't like me going to the island. Never did. Thinks it's haunted or something, a bad influence. Look, I can come over myself if you like, if you think the two of us can manage. Gotta leave Sim to manage the gas pumps. Babs is a pretty good girl but somehow she never cottoned on to the gas pumps."

"How many kids have you got, Homer?"

"Nine, counting the two she adopted."

"Gosh, that's a lot."

"You wouldn't leave a kid without a home just because you're scared of a little work."

"I would. She wouldn't. Listen, we can do it when you're not so busy."

"Monday night's not so bad. I couldn't help you on a weekend. This is the busy season, and now we've got the campground — they don't know anything, you know. Half the time not even how to light their Coleman stoves. You got to make sure they don't fill the tanks with barbecue lighter fluid. Then there's all the business of the Flushabyes going down the septic tanks. Gotta have septic tanks. What do people go camping for if they can't take their children? Some of the women spend all their time in the laundromat —

and the outboards to fix at the Marina. Gosh, some of them come up here and sit in their trailers all day drinking beer. Fishing widows. Main thing is, you can't do it no more for $2.50 a day, not with all the new regulations. Anyway, I'll be glad to get away for a bit. She'll simmer down."

She drove back, her thoughts divided. She felt she was taking a man away from his wife. She felt she was offering him something of a holiday. She was glad his wife adopted children and refused to man gas pumps, but she was angry with her raised and querulous voice. Fish wives give us all a bad name, she thought.

Fishwives. Fishwidows. And we all set out to be mermaids.

Bears were once common on the British Isles. Caledonian bears were imported by the Romans and used as instruments of torture. In Wales, it was a beast of chase.

Homer brought a bottle of rye. They had a drink, then went below and lit the lamps. He had never, he said, been "below decks" but once before, and that to bring up some lawn chairs when the old lady held a dim flashlight. He peered around fascinated. He found a stash of old lamps she had not noticed, coal-oil lamps, fancy candle-shades, even a brass student's lamp, which he coveted. Even though it was the Institute's by law, she gave it to him. Why the hell not? she thought. He's been so good to me.

One by one, they dragged the trunks up the stairs. They put some in the kitchen, some in the bedroom and the dining room. Sat down exhausted at the table.

"Well," he asked, "aren't you going to open them?"

"I guess I should." It struck her as odd that now when there was treasure trove all around her, she was not shaking.

"You should dust them, first," he said.

"I guess I should."

"You're not that kind of woman, are you?"

"What kind of woman?"

"Housekeeping first."

"Hell, no, Homer."

"You better clean 'em up before you open them. Where you've got no running water, the thing is to get at the dirt right away. Can't hose the place down, you know."

"Which one first?"

"You want me to be here?"

"If you were told to go away, would you, Homer?"

"Nope."

"The oldest or the newest?"

"That footlocker there from the first war. I was always interested in uniforms."

She found a rag and rubbed at the trunk. Not too well in case she should appear to be giving in to him. Opened the trunk. It contained two rough green-brown army blankets.

"Can't win 'em all," Homer said. "Have another smidgen of the good stuff."

Some were empty, some were full. One contained empty Gem jars and one beautiful dresses from the nineteen twenties and thirties: beaded chintzes, heavenly dark velvets, and a strange peach-coloured velveteen evening coat appliqued with silver kid. She took them into the bedroom and tried them on in front of the tall, swinging pier-glass. Homer loomed in the doorway.

"They don't go with your tan," he said.

"I don't know what to do with all my straps."

"They held their own busts up, my mother used to say."

"Nonsense, they tied them down so they could pretend they didn't have any. On the farm girls, it didn't work."

Breasts were not Homer's subject. He began to talk about the marina business. He told her more about the marina business than she would ever need to know.

"Whose were the old dresses, do you think?"

"Oh, the old Colonel's, I think. She went somewhere away to school, England, I guess, or Montreal, and she was away a long time. I heard tell once I think, only I'm not sure I remember, she took some millionaire's daughter around to parties in Europe in the good old days before the crash. In those days they didn't let the girls run loose. I guess the Colonel had good connections, so she took this girl all around and kept an eye on her. She usedta tell me something about the way they lived over there. They'd hire a plane to get from Paris to parties in London or Oxford, a little open four-seater. They had their own sheepskin jackets and leather helmets made, she said."

"Wow."

"Ah, you and me, what would we do with a butler, eh? Tip him and call him 'my man'? When I was guiding there was an old Yankee gent I liked, he was real generous, sometimes he called me 'my boy.' I told him I'd quit if he didn't call me Homer. Or Campie, sometimes they called me Campie, in those days. He understood.''

"Come on into the other room, and we'll get at the rest of the trunks."

"You know, when you're drinking, you've got to be careful of the lamps."

"I'll take the flashlight in, and you light the gas bracket for me."

"Good girl."

She did not like the parlour. It was full of wrong-angled, unlivable corners, the weakness of the octo-gon. The furniture was squared and sat ill and off-centred. Every time she went into the room, it imprinted on her the conventional rectangle and nagged. However, under the flickering light, half-hunkering against the horsehair sofa, she opened one of the trunks.

As she leaned to its mystery, Homer pinched her behind.

"Don't," she said.

"Engaged elsewhere?"

Her heart flopped. "You are," she said.

"Oh, hell, Babs and I . . . twenty-four years. If a guy can't . . ."

"If a guy can, she can."

"I'd kill her."

"Then keep your hands off me."

He stood sulkily before her now, glowering. "You asked me over."

"To help me with the trunks. As you've helped with the trunks. I didn't ask you to bring the booze, though I've enjoyed it. Let's see what's in this trunk."

He took her arm. "Look here . . ."

"Shut up, Homer." She stood and faced him. They were the same height. She was younger, he was stronger. She liked him, but she did not like what he was doing. Taking, she thought, advantage. Suddenly, she wanted to pull rank, pull class on him, keep him in his place. She knew they were equal but she did not feel they were equal, in her head she was a grand lady going to balls, he was a servant who knew her secrets.

She was still wearing, in fact, a ball gown. She looked down. There is cleavage, there are breasts half hanging out.

"Oh God, I'm sorry," she said.

Homer shook his head. "It wasn't that. I like you, you know. I like you. When I like a woman I like her no matter what she wears. Don't matter none to me if you're in jeans and a checkered shirt. Sure, I'm full of booze. A man gets a night off every once in a while. Nothing wrong with that. You like it, too, don't you? Never once turned down a drink, nor offered one. You're a snob. I never knew you were that. I should have."

She tried to hold him back. "Homer . . ."

He jammed his cap on his head. "If you want any work from now on you'll contract it through your Institute, your fucking Institute."

She stood, uncertain, then touched him. "Sit down."

"No, I'm going."

"Come into the kitchen where it's friendly and I'll put on a sweatshirt so I'm not a grand lady any more. We haven't notched the bottle yet."

"I got to go home. Babs'll be mad."

"Come and sit down . . . my man." Because the wheels were going around in her head, bells were ringing, she was understanding things.

"I like you," she said in the kitchen. "But there's Babs. And if I pay you with sex where does that leave me?"

"You got a good head," he said. "I hadn't thought of that. That bit about Babs — you leave that to me. It's our private business, see? Every man and his wife have a deal, you can't interfere with it. No way you can be good to Babs by pulling a fast one on me. She won't appreciate it. She don't care if I'm pulling trunks upstairs or screwing you, it's all the same to her. I'm just not there. She's a woman, she wants me to be there, right under her thumb. But a man's got to be away some of the time, and she don't man the gas pumps no matter what."

She was thinking, I won't ever lie back on a desk again, not ever, ever . . . .

"But," he said, "I like you. And you're living here all alone. You like to drink, I thought, well, she probably likes to screw and what's all that wrong with it? You're a modern woman, after all."

She thought, I could take him into my bed and send him off at dawn through the reeds and the kingfishers. I like him. He's hard, he's tough, he'd be good at it. I could hold him. Maybe he'd even hold me. It would be human. God knows, there might be something country boys know I never heard of. But it went against some grain in her.

"Listen," she said. "Just help me move the trunks away so there'll be a clear way through the kitchen. Anyway, I've got the curse. And I did give you some Scotch once, Homer."

She was afraid then that he'd say something unforgivable about riding the rags, but he didn't. He helped her.

"Are we still friends?" she asked.

"Sort of," he said sheepishly.

Both of them knew they had nobody to tell about this, and it made them feel better.

XVIII

"Bear," she cried. "I love you. Pull my head off." The bear did not, but her menstrual fever made him more assiduous. She was half afraid of him, but drunk and weak for danger. She took his thick fur that skidded in her hands, trying to get a grip on his loose hide, but when she went deeper into it she encountered further depth, her short nails slipped.

She cradled his big, furry, assymetrical balls in her hands, she played with them, slipping them gently inside their cases as he licked. His prick did not come out of its long cartilaginous sheath. Never mind, she thought, I'm not asking for anything. I'm not obliged to anybody. I don't care if I can't turn you on, I just love you.

The weather was at its gayest, blue and blossoming. She swam, and when the channel was empty, swam in great gusts and spurtings with the bear. She gathered bitter lettuces in the garden. She worked in the office with the canvas shades let down against the blinding sun that poured in the lantern. She went through the contents of the trunks again and again, finally slitting a blue calico cotton lining and finding Colonel Cary's letter of commission in the 49th Foot, his military citations from Portugal, a draft of a letter petitioning for ownership of the island, and a cartoon of Rowlandson's showing a man in black boots disappearing up a damsel's dress. This she thumbtacked under the Colonel's portrait. It humanized him.

Because what she disliked in men was not their eroticism, but their assumption that women had none. Which left women with nothing to be but housemaids.

She unfolded and copied his precious papers. She cleaned the house and made it shine. Not for the Director, but because she and her lover needed peace and decency.

Bear, take me to the bottom of the ocean with you, bear, swim with me, bear, put your arms around me, enclose me, swim, down, down, down with me.

Bear, make me comfortable in the world at last. Give me your skin.

Bear, I want nothing but this from you. Oh, thank you, bear. I will keep you safe from strangers and peering eyes forever.

Bear, give up your humility. You are not a humble beast. You think your own thoughts. Tell them to me.

Bear, I cannot command you to love me, but I think you love me. What I want is for you to continue to be, and to be something to me. No more. Bear.

Sometimes, late at night, she got faraway stations on her transistor radio. Garbled languages from over the pole, slow accents from New Orleans. One night when she was working by the upper window in a soft, soapy summer wind, Greek music began to flood the room. The bear snoozed by the dead fireplace. It was well after midnight. The wind riffled her papers as the bouzoukis sobbed.

"Bear," she said suddenly, "come dance with me." She stood up and began to shift her feet in the Greek pattern, holding up her arms like a Cretan figurine.

Slowly, the bear lifted himself up. She had the impression that it hurt or confused him to stand long on his hind legs, that his muscles did not obey him easily in that position, but he stood unsteadily across from her and, as she moved her feet and arms in time to the pulsing music, began slowly to bob and shuffle.

She watched him. He was wonderful. A strange, fat, mesomorphic mannikin, absurdly heavy in calf and shoulder, making his first attempt to dance upright. A baby! A wonderful half-balancing, half-smiling uncertain, top-heavy . . .

Plink, went the music. Zonk. "Ephies . . . ." You went away. No, I won't go away, she thought to him. I won't ever go away. I shall make myself strange garments out of fur in order to stay with you in the winter. I won't ever, ever, leave you.

He danced across from her. He moved a little, shifting his weight from haunch to haunch, delicately swaying his enormous feet, sawing his arms slowly in the air. She moved towards him. "Eph—ie—esss." The Greek clubs in Toronto had played that one until even an Anglo-Saxon learned a few of the words. It was a wail of loss, of loneliness. No one could fail to respond.

Whatever radio station it was saved her from distraction by switching to a more primitive record. The music was higher, more dissonant, the beat was uncertain. The bear swayed, looking to her for direction. She moved towards him and took his paws in her hands, and then, her fingers interlaced with his sets of knitting needles, began to sway against him to the music.

She had never embraced him upright. It was hot and strange. She swayed against him. She put her head on his shoulder. He stood still, very still. He did not know what to do. She remembered herself as a half child in a school gym, being held to a man's body for the first time, flushed, confused, and guilty.

He did not reciprocate her embrace. He stood very still as she moved her body as close as possible to his. Then he yawned. She felt his great jaw moving down against her face. Out of the corner of her eye she saw the gleam of his teeth, and that two of them were missing. She moved away from him. The music had turned into a strange rubbing pizzicato, rhythmic and systaltic.

The bear went down on all fours. Men began to make strange grunting noises against the violins. The bear lay down, his ears pricked to half-animal sounds. She let him rest a moment, then lay beside him. He excited her. She took off her clothes. He began his assiduous licking. He licked her armpits and the line between her breasts that smelled of sweat.

"Byron's bear danced," she whispered, "but he paid no attention. If he had known you, would the Beau have finished his days among nuns, playing with his turdies?"

Sometimes the bear half-ripped her skin with his efficient tongue, sometimes he became distracted. She had to cajole and persuade him. She put honey on herself and whispered to him, but once the honey was gone he wandered off, farting and too soon satisfied.

"Eat me, bear," she pleaded, but he turned his head wearily to her and fell asleep. She had to put a shirt on and go back to work.

She picked up an embossed volume entitled *The Poetical Works of John Milton, Volume I* published at Hartford in 1856. The illustrations and paper were mediocre, but the print was large. It struck her it would have been pleasant to read "Paradise Lost" in such type at school. It looked somehow forthright.

Out of the volume fell another message from God or Colonel Cary: *Among the Ainu of Japan, once, long ago, a bear cub was taken from its mother and raised at a woman's breast. It became a member of the village and was honoured with love and good. At the winter solstice when it was three years old, it was taken to the centre of the village, tied to a pole, and, after many ceremonies and apologies, garroted with pointed bamboo sticks. Ceremonies were again performed, during which its surrogate mother mourned for it, and its flesh was eaten.*

"Never," she cried.

115

She went out and swam naked in the black night river. Lay on her back and watched the aurora flickering mysterious green in the magic sky.

It was a hot night, very soft on the skin. The insects seemed mostly to have gone away. She fell asleep on the grass, and dreamt that Grinty and Greedy were rolling down the hill in a butter churn towards her.

"We'll eat her," Grinty said. "We'll eat her breasts off."

'You watch,"said Greedy. "You watch. She'll eat us first. Let's run."

She woke, stiff and cold and guilty. She fumbled upstairs and blew the lamps out. The bear was gone. It seemed to her human and sweet and considerate that he should take care of himself when it was time. When she went to bed, she found him in his right place. It was too hot to sleep with him.

XIX

She knew now that she loved him. She loved him with such an extravagance that the rest of the world had turned into a tight meaningless knot, except for the landscape, which remained outside them, neutral, having its own orgasms of summer weather. When there were no motorboats she now swam with the bear, swam for hours, splashing and fishing him pretty stones which he accepted gravely and held to his short-sighted eyes. On the shore, he tossed her pinecones. In the boathouse, she found a ball. They sat with their legs splayed on the grass and rolled it between them. She tried to toss it, but he seemed to be afraid, not to be able to catch it, so they rolled it gravely, hour, it seemed, after hour. Swam again. Played seal games. He swam underneath her and blew bubbles at her breasts. She spread her legs to catch them.

She knew now that she loved him, loved him with a clean passion she had never felt before. Once, briefly, she had had as a lover a man of elegance and charm, but she had felt uncomfortable when he said he loved her, felt it meant something she did not understand, and indeed, it meant, she discovered, that he loved her as long as the socks were folded and she was at his disposal on demand; when the food was exquisite and she was not menstruating; when the wine had not loosened her tongue, when the olive oil had not produced a crease in her belly. When he left her for someone smaller and neater and more energetic and subservient to his demands, she had thrown stones at their windows, written obscenities with chalk on the side of their building, obsessed herself with imagining the neatness of his young girl's cunt (he had made Lou have an abortion), dwelt on her name (though she never saw her until years later and discovered her to be quite, quite plain), carved anagrams of her rival's names on her arm, in short, surprised herself with the depths of her passionate chagrin at losing a man who was at heart petty and demanding.

For a week, she had loved the Director. For longer than that, perhaps. Certainly she had been in need of a sexual connection. Cucumbers, she had found on investigating the possibilities suggested in *Lysistrata,* were cold. Women left her hungry for men. The Director shared her interests, was charming and efficient; they had much in common when they fucked on Molesworths' maps and handwritten geneologies: but no love.

She loved the bear. She felt him to be wise and accepting. She felt sometimes that he was God. He served her. As long as she made her stool beside him in the morning, he was ready whenever she spread her legs to him. He was rough and tender, assiduous, patient, infinitely, it seemed to her, kind.

She loved the bear. There was a depth in him she could not reach, could not probe and with her intellectual fingers destroy. She lay on his belly, he batted her gently with his claws; she touched his tongue with hers and felt its fatness. She explored his gums, his teeth that were almost fangs. She turned back his black lips with her fingers and ran her tongue along the ridge of his gums.

Once and only once, she experimented with calling him "Trelawny" but the name did not inspire him and she realized she was wrong: this was no parasitical collector of memoirs, this was no pirate, this was an enormous, living creature larger and older and wiser than time, a creature that was for the moment her creature, but that another could return to his own world, his own wisdom.

She still worked. Upstairs. Slowly. *The fishermen of Newfoundland,* one of Cary's notes told her, *collect the bones of bears' pricks in the forest and pound them into the walls of their cabins to use as coathooks.* His prick was thick, protected, buried in its sheath. She got down on her knees and played with it, but it did not rise. Ah well, she thought, the summer's not over yet.

Then she discovered an immensely valuable early edition of Bewick's *Natural History* and felt justified.

They lived sweetly and intensely together. She knew that her flesh, her hair, her teeth and her fingernails smelled of bear, and this smell was very sweet to her.

"Bear," she would say to him, tempting him, "I am only a human woman. Tear my thin skin with your clattering claws. I am frail. It is simple for you. Claw out my heart, a grub under a stump. Tear off my head, my bear."

But he was good to her. He grunted, sat across from her, and grinned. Once laid a soft paw on her naked shoulder, almost lovingly.

She went to Homer's as seldom as possible now and only after swimming, in case the bear's smell carried on the air. She bought more food than she had before. When she cooked for herself she cooked also for the bear, and he sat beside her on the stoop, and sometimes he picked up his plate and licked it.

"I do wonder," wrote the Director, "whether you feel the library is good enough to warrant this investment in time."

Go screw a book, she wanted to write back to him.

She now lived intensely and entirely for the bear. They went berrying together in the woods. He pawed the ripe raspberries greedily into his maw. She saved hers like soft jewels in an old Beehive Honey tin with a bindertwine handle she found in the shed. She wished he would find a honey tree, she wanted to see him greedy among bees, but he found only worms and grubs under decaying stumps. She found wild asparagus no thicker than trillium stems and cooked it and found it delicious.

One morning she got on her hands and knees, and they shared their cornflakes and powdered milk and raspberries. Their strange tongues met and she shuddered.

The weather became very hot. He lay in his den, panting. She lay on her bed, wanting him, but it was not his time. She thought of her year as a mistress, waiting for her exigent man to come home hungry not for her but for *steak au poivre,* how she had wanted him always in the afternoon, and never dared to ask. How it might have been different, but . . .

Out on the river, water-skiers buzzed like giant dragonflies. It was too hot to work upstairs. She lay naked, panting, wanting to be near her lover, wanting to offer him her two breasts and her womb, almost believing that he could impregnate her with the twin heroes that would save her tribe. But she had to wait until night fell before it was safe to see him.

It was the night of the falling stars. She took him to the riverbank. They swam in the still, black water. They did not play. They were serious that night. They swam in circles around each other, very solemnly. Then they went to the shore, and instead of shaking himself on her, he lay beside her and licked the water from her body while she, on her back, let the stars fall, one, two, fourteen, a million, it seemed, falling on her, ready to burn her. Once she reached up to one, it seemed so close, but its brightness faded from her grasp, faded into the milky way.

Loons cried, and whippoorwills.

She sat up. The bear sat up across from her. She rose to her knees and moved towards him. When she was close enough to feel the wet gloss on her breasts, she mounted him. Nothing happened. He could not penetrate her and she could not get him in.

She turned away. He was quite unmoved. She took him to his enclosure and sent him to bed.

She dressed, and spent the rest of the night lying on the coarse marsh grass. The stars continued to fall. Always out of reach. Towards dawn, the sky produced its distant, mysterious green flickering aurora.

The next day she was restless, guilty. She had broken a taboo. She had changed something. The quality of her love was different now. She had gone too far with him. There was something aggressive in her that always went too far. She had thrown a marcasite egg at her lover's window once, a green egg she particularly valued. She had stayed in this house too long. She had fucked the Director. She had let her breasts hang out before Homer. She had gone too far. No doubt if she had children she would neglect them.

She went upstairs and found how little there was left to do. She went downstairs and masturbated. She felt empty and angry, a woman who stank of bestiality. A woman who understood nothing, who had no use, no function.

She went down to the boat and rammed around the channel like any other foolish motorized person, veering near shoals, daring the waves of the open water. But the rivers were both very calm and all she saw was the red limb of a maple tree. It made her want to die.

She went to bed without supper, without feeding the bear. In her dream, green people slid off the wind and claimed parts of her body to eat. "This is mine!

This is mine! No, that part is too old. That is too used. She has hairs on her breast. Take her away."

The horses that pulled the sun stopped and pawed. The Charioteer lashed them on. "Nor snow, now wind, nor rain," he gabbled at them. "Giddyap, Tarzan, giddyap, Tony. It's jocund day, get at it, fellas." Then when he saw the blob of flesh they were shying from, he drove the axe-edges of his wheels in another direction and there was no day in that place.

She knew she had to hide, but there was no cavity, no bear. She cooled herself in the water, curling and uncurling, flexing and unflexing, for she knew she had come from water. She sucked at her toes and fingers, pretending to be born. The waves continued to suck at the shore.

"It wasn't very witty," the Devil said in the night, "to commit an act of bestiality with a tatty old pet. An armadillo, now, might at least have been original; more of a challenge. Bestiality's all right in itself, but you have to do it with style. You've never done anything with style, have you? You're only an old kind of tarpaulin woman, you have no originality, no grace. When your lover went off with that green little girl you said the commonest sort of things, you wrote on pavements with chalk like a child, when instead you could have said he wasn't much of a catch. Then you went after the boss — fancy that, being as unimaginative as that — and when he screwed you, you made sure it wasn't on the most valuable maps. You have no pride, no sense of yourself. An abominable snowman might have been recherché, or you might had tried something more refined like an interesting kind of water-vole. The lemming's prick-bone you know, can only be seen under a magnifying glass. There's a priest in the Arctic with a collection of them; I could have told you about that, if you'd only listened. The trouble with you Ontario girls is you never acquire any kind of sophistication. You're deceiving yourself about that bear: he's about as interesting as an ottoman: as you, in fact. Be a good girl, now, and go away. No stars will fall in your grasp."

The bear came to her. His breathing was infinitely heavy and soft. She realized he was watching over her. It was morning. He must be hungry. She got up slowly and heavily and opened them both a can of beans. They ate them cold.

XX

She looked at herself in the female colonel's pier-glass. Her hair and her eyes were wild. Her skin was brown and her body was different and her face was not the same face she had seen before. She was frightened of herself.

She warmed water and washed her hair and her face in the basin. She brushed her teeth and retched at the toothpaste. She found lipstick and a comb and stuff to put on her eyes. She found a clean checkered shirt.

She got into the motorboat and went to the marina. Babs was at the counter.

"Where's Homer?" she asked.

"Up at the lumbermill, first road off past the falls. To the right," said Babs, without a second look.

She drove into the town and bought whisky. Homer was at the abandoned lumbermill, filling his pickup with firewood to sell to his campers.

"Hi."

"Long time no see."

"Been on a work-jag."

"Thought you might get bushed."

"I brought you a drink."

He grinned. "Cups?"

"I've got one in the glove-compartment."

"Me, too."

They sat on a log side by side and began to drink it straight. They kept up with each other. He had no stories to tell her. When half the bottle was gone he plucked her sleeve and took her into a decayed bunk-house. Unbuckled his belt. As she did hers. They stood half-undressed before each other. He grinned. "Can't do too long without it, can we?"

There were no preliminaries. He had a good long prick and he used it. It felt very strange and naked, and he had a way of hesitating and starting again that was unlike anything she had known before. He excited her. And it was good to have that enormous emptiness filled, but she felt nothing with him, nothing.

When he was finished he said thank you. Then they dressed.

"You keep the rest of the bottle," she said.

"No, you. It's easier for me to git."

"Well, okay. You can stop by for a drink some time."

"Sure will. Thanks."

She went home and cried. Then she went upstairs and tried to work again. Surely there was something

126

in that enormous library, surely an annotated *Roughing It in the Bush* or a journal. Something more than a recipe for raspberry shrub.

> *Otso, thou my well-beloved*
> *honey-eater of the woodlands,*
> *let not anger swell thy bosom;*
> *I have not the force to slay thee*
> *willingly thy life thou givest*
> *as a sacrifice to Northland . . .*
> *We shall never treat thee evil,*
> *thou shalt dwell in peace and plenty*
> *thou shalt feed on milk and honey . . .*
> — *The Kalevala*

"Oh God," she cried, "I was never a woman who wore circles of animals eating each other around her neck to church. I don't want his guts for my windowpanes or his shoulderblades to cut my grass. I only want to love him."

But he smelled man on her that night and would not come to her.

"People get funny up here," said Homer, "when they're too much alone. There was a Colonel who was magistrate after the first Cary. He shot the man who shot his pet beaver. Orville Willis and the Swede he had working for him spent all winter in a wickie-up over by Gardner's Reach, cutting logs for a house and eating turnips and fish. In the spring, one of the Leroys found them curled up like the Babes in the Woods, stone dead. Mrs. Francis, an English lady, and her daughter, got left alone on her no-good son Ralph's farm. They got meat-hungry and they went into the barn and caught swallows in those big nets that ladies used to wear on their hats. They plucked them and roasted them on their hatpins and said they were pretty good. There's wild hazelnuts grows around here too, they're good eating. Have another?"

She sat cross-legged away from him. He crept closer.

"You stink of bear," he said.

"I guess I do. There's no way of living with him except living close to him." She stared at Homer's hairless ears and thought of his hairless body. Shuddered.

"People get funny when they're too much alone."

"I have a lot of work to do."

"What're they going to do with the place, anyhow?"

"Use it for conferences, maybe."

"Not enough room. Sleep four at the most."

"I don't know," she said impatiently, "I don't know. I have to make a report on it, I don't know what to say."

"Turn into a fishing camp for government bigwigs more likely."

"You and Joe still want to take care of it?"

"Sure, it's a job."

When the bottle was finished she walked out to the boat with him. He handed her a stack of mail. The air was chilly.

"Fall's coming on," he said. "You'll be going soon."

"Soon, Homer."

"Joe says he's coming soon for the bear. Old Mrs. Leroy, she's none too well. They've got the extreme unction out on the coffee table all the time, now. She wants to see the bear before she goes. Joe says he reckoned the other night she must be about a hundred and four."

"Healthy climate, Homer."

"Used to be nice in the old days when all the funerals was by boat."

"I guess it was, Homer."

He went away.

XXI

After Labour Day, the motorboats miraculously disappeared. The water was beginning to be cold again, but at high noon she and the bear were able to play like otters in the water. She wound herself in her bathrobe on the bank afterwards.

She had an urge to put up preserves. Certainly there were bottles in the basement, old greenish Gem jars now worth a fortune in foolish antique stores, with corroded metal tops and stretched rubber rings. But her garden was a flop, and she spent the afternoons instead lazing in the sun with the bear, thinking of the things she would have to do if she were to stay with him all winter, thinking herself into a rugged, pastoral past that it was too late to grasp, remembering the screeching taste of fresh buttermilk, the warm milkiness of succotash and how one of her aunts made soap out of bacon grease and lye and how she burned the hired man's European frilled shirts with a flat-iron once, even though it sang when she spat on it.

She was idle and grubby. Her nails were broken. She and the bear sat in pompous idleness on the lawn. In the evening, they lazed by the upstairs fire.

Bear and woman by the fire. Both in their pelts. His thick pelt tonguing her again, her hands in his fur. The smell of him drink to her now.

Night and silence. Far away, the last lakers booming along the river. Once, a spark from a birch log landed in his fur. It smelled of burning feathers until she licked it out.

He was slower now. Losing his assiduity. He ate great quantities. She knew he was growing a plug of fat in his anus against hibernation. She was nearly — oh, really, completely — through with her work.

She was cold without his fur around her. She wriggled closed to him, closer. Until he encompassed her. He moved a leg and nearly broke her arm. She had forgotten his great weight.

"It's over, now," she told him. "It's over. You have to go to your place and I to mine." She sat up and put her sweater on.

He sat up across from her, rubbing his nose with a paw and looking confused. Then he looked down at himself. She looked as well. Slowly, majestically his great cock was rising.

It was not like a man's, tulip-shaped. It was red, pointed, and impressive. She looked at him. He did not move. She took her sweater off and went down on all fours in front of him, in the animal posture.

He reached out one great paw and ripped the skin on her back.

131

At first she felt no pain. She simply leapt away from him. Turned to face him. He had lost his erection and was sitting in the same posture. She could see nothing, nothing, in his face to tell her what to do.

Then she felt the blood running down her back, and knew she had to run away.

"Get out!" she shouted, pulling her sweater on to — well, warm her, cover it up, sop up the blood. "Get out." She drew a stick out of the fire and waved it at him. "Get out. Shoo. Time for bed. Go."

Slowly and deliberately, he got up on all fours and waddled down the stairs.

She put the screen in front of the fire. Put her jeans on. Blew out the Tilley lamp. Picked up her cigarettes and followed him down the stairs. He knocked something over in the kitchen. He'll smell my blood, he'll want me now, she thought.

"Go," she screamed. He went out through the back door, scuttling. She walked as erectly as possible to the door, bolted it, and fell shaking into bed.

When she awoke, it was still light. She was burning. She knew what had happened. She had stayed out too long in the sun, it must be the second of July, and her mother had put that stuff that was like rubber-cement on her back and she was stuck to the sheets, and chilled with sunstroke. She was going to get a fever now and vomit a lot and be taken care of and then be told she never did anything except in extremes. The only thing to do was rip herself off the muslin sheets quick, get it over with.

She struggled, She would not come loose. There was something different. She tried to raise one arm. Pain screamed. It rang in her ears. She remembered.

Oh God, I am a fool, a fool, a f . . .

It was day. The light was streaming in, She was lying stuck to the bed in full daylight. Unable to raise her left arm. Something had happened. That.

Christ have mercy upon us.

The room she lay in was dirty. Her hands were dirty. How long have I been like this? she wondered, and where is he? Is he hungry? Is it fall already? Has he gone to sleep?

She moved her legs. Good. She had clothes on, she found. She could move her head, her right arm, and, slowly, now, her left. Oh Jesus and John Wesley, it hurts. My hands are cold, my head is hot. I must get up.

She found she could roll off the bed. She found she could stand. She walked into the kitchen and found that she could walk. Drink. Take aspirin.

He ripped me, she thought. That's what I was after, wasn't it, decadent little city tart?

She leaned against the kitchen counter for a while, deciding what to do. Then she went out the front door and lay in the river in her clothes, until she felt her sweater coming loose from her broken skin.

She tried to remember what happened. She remembered him rising to her, then his one gesture. Her screams. Her flight. Had she been foolish? Oh, no. If there was enough wild animal left in him to do that, the blood . . .

The water was freezing. She got up and ran into the house. Shucked off her bottoms and, with the greatest difficulty, her top. Looked at herself naked in the great oval pier-glass once more.

She was different. She seemed to have the body of

a much younger woman. The sedentary fat had gone, leaving the shape of ribs showing. Slowly, she turned and looked over her shoulder in the pier-glass at her back: one long, red, congealing weal marked her from shoulder to buttock. I shall keep that, she thought. And it is not the mark of Cain.

She went in to the kitchen and soaked a tee shirt in disinfectant. Slung it over her shoulders for a while. Then dressed, and very slowly set about making her breakfast.

When she went outside, the bear was waiting expectantly for her. She handed him his plate. They sat quietly side by side. She shivered for a while. There was a nip in the air. He edged a little closer to her.

Upstairs, he lay and watched the play of the fire while she sat at her desk, opening the mail Homer had brought her the other day. A summer's *Times Literary Supplements* overflowing with advertisements for archivists, a number of angry letters from the Director (was he feeling sexually deprived?), a letter from her sister describing things that are of interest to mothers only but still cry out to be described.

She sat beside the bear for a while, reading. Last night she had been afraid that the smell of blood on her would cause him to wound her further, but today he was something else: lover, God or friend. Dog too, for when she put her hand out he licked and nuzzled it.

Something was gone between them, though: the high, whistling communion that had bound them during the summer. When she looked out the window, the birch trees were yellowing, the leaves were already thin.

Methodically, she began to pack her books and papers. When she had done that she would begin to clean the house.

XXII

That night, lying clothed and tenderly beside him by the fire, she was a babe, a child, an innocent. The loons' cries outside were sharp, and for her. The reeds rubbed against each other and sang her a song. Lapped in his fur, she was wrapped in a basket and caressed by little waves. The breath of kind beasts was upon her. She felt pain, but it was a dear, sweet pain that belonged not to mental suffering, but to the earth. She smelled moss and clean northern flowers. Her skin was silk and the air around her was velvet. The pebbles in the night water gleamed with a beauty that was their own value, not a jeweller's. She lay with him until the morning birds began to sing.

What had passed to her from him she did not know. Certainly it was not the seed of heroes, or magic, or any astounding virtue, for she continued to be herself. But for one strange, sharp moment she could feel in her pores and the taste of her own mouth that she knew what the world was for. She felt not that she was at last human, but that she was at last clean. Clean and simple and proud.

She went down to the water's edge and watched the miracle of the dawn. She felt the sinister pike sliding through the reeds where they belonged. She watched the last gathering summer birds, and felt the eyes of the goshawks upon her, without fear.

The water was cold on her feet, but the air was good and gracious. She turned around, and the white house behind her stood frail and simple too: no longer a symbol, but an entity.

She went in and continued to pack her tidy files.

Later in the day, a man in a red and black mackinaw, a huge man with a shock of black hair, came to the back door. He was Joe King, nephew of Lucy Leroy. He knew she was going, he said, and he and Lucy would like to take care of the bear for the winter.

Well, she thought, well. It has come. But the time felt ripe.

She enquired about Lucy's health, which was holding up.

"She'll be glad to see him. She sure is stuck on that bear. She says she don't have nobody to talk to. She hopes you made friends with him."

"I used to go swimming with him."

"He looks in good shape."

"I'm going to miss him, but I can hardly take him to Toronto."

"If we leave him here, some goddamn hunter will get him."

"You won't kill him when Lucy goes, will you?"

"Only if he's sick. We don't eat bear paws any more. Anyways, Lucy will make us promise. You don't have to fear."

She went up to him and gently put his chain on.

"Lucy said you'd get on good with him," Joe said.

"Oh, I got on good with him. He's a fine fellow."

"When are you going back to Toronto?"

"In a couple of days. I have to leave the house in good shape. And there are a few last papers to deal with."

"I don't suppose you found any buried treasure. They didn't know much, people like the Carys. They were tourists."

"Compared to you and Lucy."

She walked with them down to the dock. Then she went back and got the remains of the chow for them. When she returned, the bear was already ensconced in the motorboat, quite contented. She rubbed his ruff affectionately, and scratched his small gristly ears.

"Good-bye," she said.

Joe started the motor. The bear twitched at the noise and his tongue flung out sideways and licked her hand. Then Joe pushed off with a casual good-bye and she was left standing, watching the bear recede down the channel, a fat dignified old woman with his nose to the wind in the bow of the boat. He did not look back. She did not expect him to.

She swept out the house, packed her belongings, and took her gear to her car in stages. She left the Cary laundry in town, including the blooded sheets,

138

in Homer's name. She went to the bank and drew out enough money to settle Homer's enormous account.

She went back and sat in the empty, enormous house. She had not found its secrets. It was a fine building, but it had no secrets. It spoke only of a family who did not want to be common clay, who feared more than anything being lost to history. With their fine tables and velvet pelmets and pier-glasses, the English wives had proclaimed their aristocracy among these Indian summer islands.

Much good it did them, she thought, perishing in the wilderness. Colonel Jocelyn was the only one who knew anything: how to tan a lynx.

Up in the office, she took the Rowlandson print down from the wall: it belonged to a time of her life that was long gone. She dusted the books and locked the cabinets. Against the regulations, she wrapped both the first edition of *Wacousta* and the Bewick in *Times Literary Supplements* to take away. Some winter, snowmobilers would break in. They would take the telescope for its brass screws, and smash the celestial and terrestial globes. Well, let the world be smashed: that was the way things were bound to go. The bear was safe. She would make these two books safe.

Over her collection of Cary's notes she hesitated. They seemed to belong more to her than to the Institute. But in the end, she put them in an envelope and left them in the desk drawer marked "Cary's notes on bears." She did not need them any more.

There was an immense peace in performing these duties, which she did thoroughly and well. She makes her little house to shine, she thought.

She stood in the tree crow's nest and took a last farewell of Cary's impressive view. She went to the beaver pond where she had never seen a beaver. The goshawks were gone. She surveyed the ruin of her garden. She stood in the doorway of the bear's old byre and inhaled his randy pong. Really, she thought, really.

It was late afternoon when she had cleaned out the kitchen, leaving a few canned goods for passers-by and a clean counter, and carried the last of her things to the boat. The river was choppy, for an autumn wind had sprung up. She went up the river slowly. She felt tender, serene. She remembered evenings of sitting by the fire with the bear's head in her lap. She remembered the night the stars fell on her body and burned and burned. She remembered guilt, and a dream she had had where her mother made her write letters of apology to the Indians for having had to do with a bear, and she remembered the claw that had healed guilt. She felt strong and pure.

Leaving the keys at Homer's, she had a farewell drink with him over the counter, away from Babs' eyes. He promised to put the shutters on the windows and look after the place all winter and bill the Institute.

"Lucy'll die happy now she has that bear back," he said.

"He's a good bear."

"I guess he is. I wouldn't know myself."

She remembered the odd ridge of Homer's upper plate the day she made love to him.

"Well, good-bye." Shaking his hand. "Thanks for everything. I didn't make much of a go of the garden."

"You did all right. You'll be up again?"

"I don't think so. I'm thinking of changing jobs. Time to move along."

"Come for a holiday. I'll give you a special rate on a tent-site."

"Thanks, Homer."

She drove south all night, taking the long, overland route. She wore a thick pullover and drove with the windows open until the smell of the land stopped being the smell of water and trees and became cities and gas fumes. It was a brilliant night, all star-shine, and overhead the Great Bear and his thirty-seven thousand virgins kept her company.

Afterword

BY ARITHA VAN HERK

Bear shuffles its ursine way into every reader's memory, an unforgettable novel. It is as quintessentially Canadian as snow, and as complicated. It's been called an outrage, it's been called pornography, it's been called pastoral, mythological, gothic, none of which quite manages to say what this book does. It explodes, in as slow and tranced a way as is possible: it is a book that explodes between the reader's hands, into the reader's head.

A woman and a bear: a bear and a woman. Alone at last. *Bear* broke through what was, until its publication, a hegemonic male/female dichotomy. That female characters in Canadian novels sought a completion to or understanding of themselves in relation to men was a given. That a heroine might come to an understanding of herself without the generic presence of man or men was barely a consideration. And when Marian Engel suggested that a bear and a woman alone were enough for any number of epiphanies, the motif of the woman who comes to terms with herself and her life was forever altered.

Even prudish readers must admit that a literal reading of *Bear* is tremendously exciting. The sexual and intellectual tensions in the novel are handled brilliantly, with deftness and finesse. The very brevity of the book (a perfect novella) speaks to its physical pleasure, and the timespan of the story (one brief summer) enriches the sensual intensity it projects. Woman and bear: bear and woman. Alone at last.

Engel said that she wanted to write a love story and when she opened the door for the lover, a bear lumbered into the room. A too literal reader might think that the woman so sweetly and assiduously licked by the bear is bestial, immoral, and depraved, but it is important to remember that the imagination lives in any metaphor of love. Yet *Bear* makes everything literal. One cannot love satisfactorily without first loving oneself. And the bear, for all its physical bearishness, is a mirror to the woman, Lou, just as she, in her animal humanness, is a mirror to the bear.

We have yet to develop an adequate language to write about love, and that statement contains its own problem. Almost every novel, every poem that chooses love as its subject is *about* love, when what is needed is a writing *of* love, not subjective or objective, but an entering, a presence within the ineffable experience. By choosing the bear as lover, Engel takes a step toward that writing. She rejects the simplicity of human sexual opposition, and instead enters the animal presence of sexuality inside the human.

A large part of all sexual presence resides inside the head, and in *Bear*, Lou is enabled finally to explore what is inside her own head through other heads. Pennarth, the name of the Carey estate, means bear's head. The house on Carey's Island is a classic Fowler's octagon, designed to emulate the structure of the brain. Lou regards it as a phrenological absurdity, given that it is too elaborate and too hard to heat, yet within the green and swimming light of the upper storey, its library typical of a nineteenth-century mind, she comes at last to know her own mind.

It is part of the mystical acrostic of this novel that, remote from the ordinary world, away from the civilized city, Lou returns to her animal self through a highly refined collection of books epitomizing the rational nineteenth century. The collection, although fine, is relatively useless as historical or scholarly information. "You do not come to northern Ontario to study London in 1825." Or, wonders Lou mischievously, do you? Is northern Ontario truly the place to sort through the detritus of post-Victorian morality and classification? Given the extent to which we are all subject to that pre-twentieth century, with its ordered (and disordered by Darwin) universe, Colonel Carey's library presents itself as the perfect place within which to experience a crisis of the self.

Through the accusation of the magnificent material at Pennarth, Lou recognizes the essential meaninglessness of her life as an archivist, a cataloguer, someone who shuffles cards, irrelevant. Eunuch-like, she watches the events in other lives unfold, but does not live herself. She has been a part of no great passion, no determined quest. At the beginning of the novel we are told that she lives like a mole, burrowed deep in the ground, surrounded by the detritus of other people's lives. She works as an archivist for "the Historical Institute," but her institutionalization goes deeper than her employment. So long as she remains there, she will be a scurrying, buried animal, forever taking inventory.

Lou's recognition that she has sacrificed human contact, that she has followed no dream, no adventure, that she is irrelevant to history and to herself, is played out against her discovery of the bear, the living part of the Carey bequest. The bear is a strange kind of ursomorphic chameleon: he is a lump, a defeated middle-aged woman, a fur-coat, a racoon, a near-sighted baby, a king, a woodchuck, a large-hipped woman, a rug, a dog, a groundhog, a man, a mesomorphic mannikin, a baby, a lover, a God, and finally, as he is taken away, a fat dignified old woman. Lou discovers that she can paint any face on him she wants, and, locked within his animal mystery, he will oblige. She has, at long last, a playfellow who does not demand of her any extraordinary subservience, any shared delusions. His entrance into the house frightens her at first, but when it is clear that he knows his way inside, she permits him to stay, and her further explorations inside the glass-enclosed brain-configured house are accompanied by the bear, who has figuratively entered

Lou's head as well. When she opens the door to him, she always expects him to be someone else, and that persistent visualization of transformation underscores the bear's role as midwife to Lou's transformation.

The thirteen slips of paper that fall out of the books Lou catalogues all contain esoteric information on bears – their physiology and mythology, their relationship to humans. Although Lou denies wanting to cast an *I Ching* for herself out of them, her careful recording of the times and dates when, as well as the page and the book where, she finds each slip suggests that this unnecessary cataloguing is her bringing together of occupation and desire. She wonders if the bear, like the books, knows generations of secrets, but she does not recognize that she has finally permitted passion to enter bibliography. The bear has walked not only into her life and into her house, but into her head, and there enacts the transfiguration that permits Lou to love herself. Loving the bear, Lou finally loves herself. Lou and the bear are one, halves of the same being. Inside the head, that country of the imagination, anything can happen, all boundaries dissolve. Women and bears can be lovers. Alone at last.

And after all, the bear is only a projection of Lou herself, that daft and middle-aged woman baffled by the complex disappointments of life, waiting for someone to open the door and enter: book, bear, lover.

It is no accident that the bear comforts Lou's solitary desolation – by making love to her (quite explicitly) with his tongue – in the library, that in the glass-enclosed upper regions of the intellect, he introduces to her the idea that she is entitled to desire. But it is also important that the bear, inhabitant of Lou's imagination, permits her to love herself, without guilt or masturbatory convenience. Lou sheds her old, imprisoned self: in the basement, she finds "the long-decayed form of a burrowing animal." She knows that she will never lie back for sex without desire again. Her old life, with its compromises and duties and guilts, is over.

Lou's exploration of eroticism, that secret territory forbidden to women, is carried out with the bear in her head as a guide. Their bestial exchange is slow and erotic and unexploitive. The bear has nothing to gain from Lou and Lou has nothing to gain from the bear: this mutuality enables them to undertake an exploration separate from the structured and power-defined male/female relationships of the world. They are both freed from their chains and can take pleasure in their natural desires.

And yet, their very freedom from expectation demarcates the line between them: one is human, one animal. Although the bear can offer Lou eroticism and sexual affirmation, he cannot be her lover, physically or otherwise. He does not turn into a prince. He stays bear. And when Lou wants to force past that boundary, when she presents herself to the bear as mate, he rips her back from shoulder to buttock, in a physical language as definitive and articulate as words and books and ideas never are. Thus, he completes what was begun: the bear who walked into her head leaves, walks itself back into the impenetrable body of bear. The scar that she will bear affirms that Lou knows at last what the world is for.

Our discomfort with *Bear* is an index of the extent to which we have incorporated, listened to, and loved the animal within. If we can learn to live with that animal, that shaggy and suggestive beast, we can come clean; we will not permit a civilized bestiality to exploit us. The acceptance of its presence suggests a wholeness and happiness that our contemporary denial of the erotic and animal self has buried.

While Engel suggests that because we have subverted honest desires there is a great and angry rift between men and women, she does offer a healing recognition. It is possible, if we love ourselves, to love others. If we dare to read what is inside the head, we might unearth the body.

A woman and a bear: a bear and a woman. Alone at last.

BY MARIAN ENGEL